CAN'T STAND THE HEAT

LEIGHANN DOBBS

LISA FENWICK

LEIGHANN DOBBS PUBLISHING

1

———

Sarah Thomas stared at the sea of expectant faces and wondered how the hell she was going to pull this off. She wasn't very good at lying. Never had been. But now here she was, a contestant in one of the world's most prestigious cooking challenges, telling the biggest lie of her life. *On television!*

A bead of sweat trickled down her forehead and onto the bridge of her nose. She swiped at it, trying to calm the pounding of her heart as she waited for the judges to announce the first challenge.

She made a mental note to kill her best friend, Marly, for talking her into this. Sure, entering the Chef Masters Challenge was a great opportunity to showcase her culinary skills as well as win some much-needed money, but the opportunity came with one gigantic problem—Raffe Washburn.

Marly had forgotten to give her one teensy-tiny detail

when she'd practically forced her to fill out the application. All the contestants had to be married or engaged. Sarah had learned that tidbit *after* she had agreed to appear on the show. It was a team effort, two people per team, and they had to be in a committed relationship, something Sarah definitely had no interest in.

Raffe was the best friend of Sarah's boss, Jasper. She supposed she knew him a bit socially because Marly was now engaged to Jasper. They'd had dinner at Jasper's a few times. But Sarah had always cooked. She'd always felt a little out of place eating with the three of them and had made excuses to spend most of her time fussing in the kitchen.

She barely knew Raffe. But she had agreed to the contest because the half-a-million-dollar grand prize was too enticing to pass up. Sarah wasn't greedy. The money wasn't for her, but it would help her solve another problem—one she was desperate to resolve. And besides, what was the worst that could happen? She and Raffe would pretend they were engaged, and no one would know any better.

Her gaze shifted from the crowd to the cooking station in front of her. Identical to the twelve other stations in the vast room, it gleamed with stainless steel from the counters to the appliances to the utensils. Her anxiety ratcheted up a notch. In mere seconds, she'd be cooking the most important meal of her life. This meal was part of the elimination challenge that would decide if she moved on to the main contest or got eliminated.

More than half the entrants would be going home today.

Her gaze drifted from the kitchen to the judging station in front of her and then back to the crowd of people who all seemed to be staring directly at her. There were a lot of people out there.

"Attention, chefs!" Landon Barkley, the celebrity host and one of the three judges, announced. "You have approximately sixty minutes to make a dish that you feel represents New York City. This can be any dish at all, but if it doesn't make us all feel like it's roots came from NYC then you're disqualified and will not move on in the competition. The challenge starts... *now!*"

The room exploded into utter chaos.

Sarah glanced at Raffe. Cheesecake. That was the first thing that popped into her head. New York-style cheesecake.

"What are you thinking? Pizza?" Raffe asked her, putting his apron on and handing one to her. "You know, New York-style pizza?"

Sarah frowned as she grabbed the apron. Was he joking? Pizza? Good grief. That would be the last thing she'd suggest they prepare unless they were sitting around watching a football game.

"I was actually thinking about cheesecake. You know, New York-style. I'm a little worried about the resting time, but I can put it in the freezer to cool it down much faster. Come on, we need to get going!" She jogged toward their pantry, Raffe following right behind her.

She stopped short, causing him to bump into her. They looked like idiots. When she had said "come on," she hadn't meant for him to tailgate her.

"Can you just pull all the equipment we need together while I grab the ingredients?" she asked then, at his confused look, added, "You know, like pots and pans. Spatulas. Whisks."

Even though Raffe was the owner of several five-star restaurants he didn't have as much cooking experience as Sarah. As the boss, he spent most of his days behind the desk, not in the kitchen. Marly had explained that the contest was important to Raffe, not only to get some hands-on experience, but also so he could become known for his skills. He wanted to prove himself. And because he didn't have much experience, he needed Sarah to help him.

Because of this, Sarah assumed Raffe realized that she should be the lead cook. But his actions and comments in the few encounters they'd had leading up to today had started to make her wonder if he didn't think otherwise. She supposed he was an *okay* cook, but he just wasn't at the level he needed to be to win the contest on his own. Too bad his big, fat ego appeared to be getting in the way of him realizing it.

She scurried off to the pantry and grabbed what she needed. Sugar, butter, graham crackers. She ran back out front to Raffe, placing the ingredients on the counter in front of him.

"You can make a crust from this, right?" She shot over

her shoulder as she ran back to the pantry for more ingredients.

"Of course!" Raffe yelled back at her, already starting on the crust.

Was that a tinge of sarcasm in his voice? It had been an honest question. She really didn't know how much he knew about baking or making crusts.

She shrugged it off and started to get the rest of the ingredients. Cream cheese, sour cream, oh look! Fresh berries. She scooped them up to add on top. She hurried back to Raffe, who already had the graham cracker crust done and in the oven.

"Okay, I'll get started mixing the rest," she said, putting the cream cheese in a large mixing bowl.

"Where are the eggs?" Raffe asked, looking around the counter then picking up a dish towel and looking under it.

"Ugh! I forgot the damn eggs. Can you...?"

"Already on my way!" Raffe replied, halfway to the pantry.

Sarah shoved a paddle blade into the mixer and turned it on. Darn thing was loud. Hopefully it wasn't some older model that was going to crap out on her. That was the last thing she needed.

"I can't find them." Raffe's voice behind her pulled her attention away from the mixer. Was he that inept he couldn't find eggs? No. She probably just misunderstood what he'd said because the mixer was so loud.

She scrunched up her face and turned to look at

him. "What?"

"I can't find the eggs!" He practically screeched at her.

Sarah refrained from rolling her eyes as she stepped back from the mixer and motioned for him to step in and take her place. Did she have to do *everything* herself? "You watch this. I'll get them."

She stomped off to the pantry. They were already cutting it close with time, and now he couldn't find the eggs? How hard could it be? The pantry was not very big. She walked inside, heading toward the small refrigerated section.

No eggs.

Her stomach fluttered uncomfortably. Don't panic. Eggs are a staple in every kitchen. They had to be here.

"Forty-five minutes!" one of the judges yelled.

Rising on her toes, Sarah looked on top of the freezer, thinking maybe for some bizarre reason the eggs were there. No luck. She spun around, anxiety surging.

Were they on the shelf with the spices? No. In with the flour and sugar? No. She scoured every shelf, pushing things out of the way, sending boxes clattering to the floor. No eggs. She ripped open the fridge door and checked again. Skunked.

Raffe was right. There were no eggs.

"Well?" Raffe asked as Sarah came flying back to the cooking station.

Sarah wasn't sure what to do. Her eyes jerked to the clock. They'd already used up a lot of the time. She was lightheaded and dizzy. Maybe she needed a paper bag to breathe in or to sit down and put her head between her knees. Raffe just stood there looking at her. How could he be so calm?

"There are no eggs. Maybe this is part of the challenge?" She craned her neck to see what the contestants next to them were cooking. A pile of egg shells sat on their counter, and five beautiful oval eggs nestled in an egg carton just beyond reach, as if taunting her.

Sarah's heart sank. They'd been given the contest rules, and talking to other contestants was a big no-no. She couldn't ask them for eggs, and she couldn't make cheesecake without eggs.

"What do we do?" Raffe asked, still mixing the cream cheese and blending in the sugar.

Sarah closed her eyes for a minute, thinking of what else they could make in the time remaining.

"Waldorf salad and New York strip steak. I know we have the ingredients." She was running to the pantry before the words were even out of her mouth.

When she returned she could tell by the look on Raffe's face that he wasn't so sure about this dish.

"Well, I don't know." His voice trailed off as he looked around.

"Raffe, we have less then forty-five minutes to make this! What else do you suggest we do?" Sarah asked, tossing the bowls and mixer filled with the beginnings of a cheesecake under the counter top. The tangy sweet smell wafted up. Too bad; it smelled good. Probably would have gone over great with the judges too.

"What if we made New York-style pizza?"

Sarah stopped short. Here we go with pizza again! No! Did he not trust her judgement? Jeez!

"Raffe, I think we need to have a really great dish for the first challenge, and this is going to be kick-ass if you can start helping me!"

"I'll make the salad. Is that okay?" he asked, starting to do it anyway.

Sarah didn't reply. She didn't know if he was a control freak or didn't trust her judgement or what. She only wanted to finish this dish on time without having a heart attack.

"*Twenty minutes!*" Sarah practically jumped out of her skin as Landon yelled the time remaining.

She looked around at their area. Okay, the steak was cooking, and the butter garlic sauce was done. Raffe was finishing up the salads after having just grabbed the apples, and they actually looked pretty impressive. Something seemed to be missing, though. Walnuts! There was no way she could present a Waldorf salad without walnuts.

"I'll grab the walnuts for the salad!" Sarah yelled, already running to the pantry. Once inside she made a beeline for the shelf where she had seen nuts. Hmm. Peanuts. Almonds. Where were the walnuts? She knew she had seen them. Cashews. Macadamias. No walnuts.

"*Five minutes!*" Landon bellowed, causing a fresh wave of panic to squeeze her chest.

She pushed items off the shelf, desperate to find the

walnuts, but they weren't anywhere to be found. She stood back, sweat dripping, chest heaving. Five bins of fruit sat on the bottom shelf. Maybe the walnuts had fallen in there.

She rummaged through. No walnuts, but she did notice there were two varieties of apples sitting in a bin, with a third section that was empty. Only the Cortland and Red Delicious apples were left, and both bins looked full.

Her chest squeezed tighter. Red Delicious apples were the type used in Waldorf salad. Raffe had grabbed the wrong apples!

Running back to their station, she grasped Raffe's elbow.

"I can't find the walnuts! They are gone! And you used the wron—"

"*Time!*" The judges yelled in unison, cutting Sarah off. "Stop what you're doing and step back from your dishes!"

Sarah's eyes darted from Raffe to the dishes he'd plated on their counter. Everything looked amazing. Everything except the salad that was missing the walnuts. And had the wrong apples.

"Okay, Team One, Sarah and Raffe, what do you have for us?" Landon asked as he approached them, looking at their dishes.

Sarah's heart swooped, her mind whirling at a way to salvage this. "Um…"

"We have a Waldorf salad with a New York strip steak." Raffe spoke up and Sarah felt a small measure of relief. He was definitely a better spokesman. He had an air of confidence and authority about him that made people pay attention when he spoke. Men, women, heck, even babies shut up when Raffe started to talk. His good looks didn't hurt either.

"Excellent. What an excellent idea." Landon said, jotting down something in a note pad. Sarah's shoulders relaxed. He hadn't mentioned the missing walnuts or the wrong apple! Maybe they would get a pass.

"*I* have a question, Team One," a voice piped up from behind Landon.

Sarah's shoulders tensed, tighter this time. The voice was that of Franz Durkin. He was a tough judge known for his harsh critiques and caustic manner. He was also a well-known food critic in New York who had been rumored to make more than one five-star chef cry.

Sarah stared intently at him, waiting for the question.

Durkin's eyes scanned their plates, coming to rest on the salad. He leaned forward and squinted.

Was he looking at the apples or searching for the missing walnuts? Did it matter? Either way it would be points off, probably enough to eliminate them. Raffe's stupid mistake had just cost her half of the half-million-dollar prize.

But maybe... just maybe, he was going to ask something else. Sarah held her breath, sending up a silent prayer.

"Hmmm," Durkin's eyes flicked from the salad to Sarah and then to Raffe. "My question is…"

2

"...Whose brilliant idea was it to dispense with the walnuts and use the Cortland apple instead?"

"That was my idea." Raffe spoke up, hoping that Sarah wouldn't pass out. She didn't seem like she was breathing, and her face had grown crimson. Not surprising given how wound up she got about things. He couldn't understand why. She was a top-notch chef, yet she didn't exactly exude confidence about her cooking. No problem. Raffe had enough confidence for them both.

"I opted to put just the apples on in place of the walnuts as I used an apple that has a much different flavor than the traditional Red Delicious. Cortland apples have a sweet, almost tangy taste, and they originate from New York. In fact, they date back to..."

"1898," Durkin finished Raffe's sentence. "Excellent work, Team One. I love this idea. This, *this* is what it's all about! Going away from the norm is good at times. Love the creativity. Very clever, Raffe." Durkin practically jumped up and down with excitement.

Raffe's mind raced. He had taken a chance and added the wrong apples on purpose, something he had learned from the weeks of research he had conducted on food pairings while preparing for this contest. That was his forte—research and thinking problems through. That's how he'd built an empire of five-star restaurants. Well, that and his father's money.

Thoughts of his father's money dampened the exhilaration Raffe had felt at Durkin's compliment. Though he had to admit the money had helped build his career, it hadn't given him any sense of accomplishment. That's why this contest was so important to him. His dream was to be recognized as a first-rate chef, and this was the one way he could prove to himself—and to the world—that he had achieved that on his own, without his father's money or influence.

The only problem was that his cooking skills weren't yet finely honed. That and the fact that the contest required quick thinking. Raffe wasn't so good at thinking on his feet. That's why he'd crammed in all that research ahead of time.

The research had paid off too. He knew those Cortland apples would add a unique twist to the salads, and they originated in New York.

He'd figured Sarah had thought he had grabbed the wrong ones by the way she'd been shooting daggers at him. He shot a smirk in her direction. Maybe this would show her he wasn't some rich loser wanting to take advantage of her culinary expertise for his own gain. True, he needed her expertise to help win the contest, but he wanted to do it on his own merits too. He wanted them to be a team.

Raffe snuck a look at Sarah out of the corner of his eye as the judges made their way down the line critiquing the other teams' dishes. Her body had lost that rigid stance, and a wisp of blond hair had worked loose from the tight bun. The brilliant overhead lights gave her amber eyes a golden glow. Standing there beside him she was almost… pretty.

Sarah turned to look at him, and Raffe jerked his head away. The *last* thing he needed was to become involved with Sarah. A fake engagement was involvement enough.

The judges had made their rounds and were now standing at the judging station. Beside him, Sarah stiffened. Raffe's heartbeat kicked up a notch, reminding him of how important this contest was to him.

Landon Barkley clapped his hands. "Chefs! You've all done a wonderful job, but as you know, only six teams will earn a place in the challenge."

Landon paused dramatically. The crowd murmured. Raffe shifted on his feet.

"For this elimination challenge, the contestants were tasked with creating a dish that epitomizes New York cuisine." Landon stopped for another annoying pause, then his gaze slowly swept over the teams as he said,

"And while some did an excellent job, others fell far from the mark."

Raffe's heart leapt. Had Landon's gaze lingered on Raffe when he said "far from the mark?" Why doesn't he just get on with it and announce the winners?

"And now… I will announce the winners…"

The room fell silent. Sarah and Raffe stood still as statues, the hot lights beating down on them. Sarah's hand brushed against his, soft and warm. Raffe held his breath.

"Congratulations, Teams One, Three, Six, Seven, Ten, and Twelve! You will move on to the next round!"

Relief flooded through Raffe. He exhaled in a loud whoosh. He raised his palm for a high five and turned toward Sarah.

SARAH COULD HARDLY BELIEVE her ears. They were in!

Raffe was already holding his palm up for a high five, and she slapped it enthusiastically with her own. Their eyes locked for a second before she was blinded as the stadium lighting sparked off her fake engagement ring— a gargantuan princess cut diamond replica.

She ripped her hand away and shoved it into her pocket. Not only was the ring's ostentatious presentation embarrassing, it was a reminder of how she was cheating to win this contest. Normally a painfully honest person, Sarah let the fact that her entry into the Chef Masters

Challenge wasn't exactly on the up and up cut her to the core. But this wasn't about her. She'd have to set aside her code of ethics if she wanted to help the one person who mattered to her the most.

Guilt washed over her. What would her parents think? She could never tell them she'd faked being engaged to get into a contest. The only saving grace was that the television show wouldn't be aired until a few months after the contest. Yes, her folks would be mad about this engagement they'd never heard of, but she'd already concocted a way to explain it; she was waiting to tell them as a surprise, but in the end things didn't work out. If they knew the real reason she had agreed to do this, they might understand, but she'd deal with that later. *After* they won.

Did they have a real chance of winning? Sarah had to admit she'd been beginning to worry about that, but then Raffe made that brilliant move with the apples, something she herself would never have considered.

"How did you know about the apples?" she asked, wiping a cloth over the stainless steel blades of their chef's knives as Raffe cleaned the countertop.

Raffe shrugged. "I did a lot of research on different types of dishes before we came here. I mean, I've eaten a lot of different foods all over the world, but I wanted to learn more about what foods draw what flavors, where they originated from, that kind of thing."

Impressive. Obviously this contest meant more to him than she had initially thought. Why would a guy like

Raffe, who already had more money than he needed and the prestige of several five-star restaurants, even care about a contest like this? She had feared that it was just a lark for him and that he wouldn't take his role seriously. She was relieved to think she might have been wrong.

"Well, you did great research then. But I would still like to know where the walnuts went!"

Raffe stopped cleaning and glanced toward the pantry. "I thought I saw walnuts in the pantry too, but maybe we were both wrong. Things moved pretty fast."

Sarah shook her head. "I'm positive I saw them. It just makes no sense. And what happened to the eggs?"

"Well, it doesn't matter anymore, so don't worry. They restock the pantries after every contest, so we should be fine."

Sarah put her knives carefully into the case, suddenly feeling drained. The anxiety of the day had taken its toll, and now she was exhausted.

Going back to her dumpy little hotel with the gold shag carpeting and crawling between the sheets suddenly seemed like heaven. She'd had to scramble to get the money together to fly out to Namara, the tropical island hosting the competition, and find accommodations. Raffe had offered to pay, but she'd refused. She didn't need anyone taking care of her. The one-story motel near the airport, with its neon sign missing half the letters, was the best she could afford.

Raffe was probably staying at the Ritz Carlton on the beach. She'd been worried about someone catching on that they weren't staying at the same hotel, but everything had been a whirlwind, and no one had had time to dig into living arrangements so far.

"So umm… I guess we should walk out together." Raffe stood at her side, his black canvas knife case in hand.

Sarah glanced around at the other teams, most of whom were finishing with the cleaning and starting to gather their things. Worry gnawed at her gut. What if people wanted to get friendly? Would she be able to pretend she was Raffe's fianceé? What if someone was staying at her hotel and noticed Raffe wasn't there?

"Yeah, I think we need to come up with some sort of plan to make it look as if we are staying together or—"

"Attention!" Landon's voice boomed across the room. "We have a surprise for those of you moving on in the competition."

Everyone turned toward Landon, who stood in front of the bank of cooking stations looking quite pleased with himself.

A surprise? Maybe a cash bonus? Or a car? Sarah glanced at Raffe, who shrugged.

"We know all of you have had to lay out a significant sum to travel here and are scattered in hotels all around the island."

The other contestants nodded and murmured. Sarah's gut tightened. What was Landon getting at?

Landon continued, "And because we want you all to

focus on food and not finances, our wonderful producers have arranged accommodations for you."

Sarah's brows shot up, and she glanced at Raffe again. Whatever they'd arranged would probably be an upgrade from where she was staying but possibly a downgrade for Raffe.

Sarah's spirits lifted as Landon clapped his hands and rubbed them together. He was clearly eager to let them in on the location, so it must be some place good. "You'll all now be staying at the Casa Del Mara Resort. We have rented half of the resort, and you will all be staying in *your own romantic bungalow!*"

Sarah's heart crashed.

Romantic bungalow? This had disaster written all over it.

VERONICA ST. JAMES' face soured at Landon's announcement about the bungalows. It may have been a surprise to the contestants, but it was old news to her.

Everyone gets a romantic bungalow, blah blah blah. Romance. Who needs that? She had never had a boyfriend. Ever. And she didn't care! She stuffed the jar of walnuts into her desk drawer and reached for her cell phone to call Tanner and tell him the bad news.

"Things didn't go as planned. They made the cut to the main contest," she said as soon as he answered, cutting right to the point. Veronica liked to avoid pleasantries at all costs.

"What? Well you messed that up, didn't you? You made it sound like a sure thing, that you had taken care of it and they wouldn't make it."

"I wasn't aware that Raffe knows how to cook as well as he does," she replied dryly, gripping a package of M&M's in her hand. She'd been certain that paying the staff member to take the eggs from their kitchen when no one was looking and stealing the walnuts from their pantry would have been enough to screw up their meal. She wouldn't underestimate them again.

"Well, make sure you stop them. I pulled in a favor to get you that job. You'd better not make me regret it."

Veronica popped a yellow M&M into her mouth, chewing it slowly. The M&M package crinkled as her grip on the bag tightened with every word Tanner said.

She didn't need *him* to prod her to make sure Sarah and Raffe didn't win this contest. She wanted them to lose more than anyone. She wanted revenge.

That nosey, plain Jane Sarah had to have been involved in her getting fired from her last job. And Raffe, well, if he preferred to be with mousey Sarah, then so be it. When did they get engaged anyway? Must have been a whirlwind romance. And why would someone like Raffe want to be in this contest? Everyone knew he had plenty of money. Neither of them deserved to win.

"How's business?" she interrupted, sick of listening to Tanner whine about her failed attempt.

"It's good. Better every day. I am counting on you to ensure it stays that way. Make sure these two don't advance again."

Veronica rolled her eyes. She had a bit of a history with Tanner Durcotte. Not in a romantic way. It was more of a shared vendetta kind of way. Sarah had had a role in screwing them both, and they both wanted to see her fail.

But Tanner also had a business reason. He owned a few restaurants in New York City that competed with Raffe's. Those restaurants were now his sole source of income thanks to Sarah and her fat friend Marly West ruining his fashion design business. He simply could not afford for Raffe to win this contest. The prestige could give Raffe's restaurants an edge.

"I think we both know I want them to fail as badly as you do, Tanner. I'll be in touch." Veronica ended the call, grabbed a few more M&M's, and started to work on her plan to bring down Team Raffe and Sarah.

3

There were worse gigs than working cleanup for the big TV show that had come to Namara Island for filming, TJ thought as he sprayed down the pots and pans before placing them on the rack that would feed them automatically into the giant dishwasher.

The cleanup room, as he called it, was quiet. No one ever came here. It was usually just him and the hum of machinery. He liked it that way. No pressure. Nobody bugging him. The job was simple. Maybe years ago he would have been disgusted with it, but now he was grateful.

"Are you almost done? Those need to be back to the set. Why does it take so long to wash this stuff? This isn't rocket science, for crying out loud!"

He cringed as soon as he heard the screeching voice. *Almost* no one bugging him. Turning around, he saw Veronica, the always-stressed blond show organizer.

The irony was amusing. He had left New York City for several reasons, the main one being to escape stress. He had needed to be someplace where there wasn't a lot of pressure. Where he could recover without people constantly pulling at him. Not to mention that he'd had to disappear for a while until he'd made good on a debt. What better place than Namara Island?

Several months ago he'd managed to scrape together the money for a cheap summer flight, and he'd never looked back. He didn't have anything or anyone keeping him in New York, and this island was the perfect place for him to pull his life back together. Except now this woman was driving him nuts every ten minutes.

"I thought the next taping wasn't until tomorrow?" he asked her, knowing that would send her into yet another tizzy.

"*You listen to me!*" she screeched at him. "Get all that cookware clean and back to the set in fifteen minutes, or I will make sure it's the last thing you do. The whole reason you have this oh-so-illustrious job is because of this production team. So move it!"

TJ smirked as he watched her turn and stalk away, her ample hips swaying. Veronica St. James bugged the crap out of him, and she was wound way too tight for his liking, but still there was something about her that he kind of liked.

Maybe it was just his natural instinct of wanting to save those he could see heading for disaster. Or maybe not. Either way, he had enough of his own problems to deal with to spend any time worrying about Veronica St. James.

SARAH FIDGETED in the back seat of the cab as it pulled through the tall scrolling black wrought iron gates of the Casa Del Mara Resort. She wondered if Raffe was already here and how they would manage to pull off living together in a romantic bungalow.

The thought of mingling with the other contestants at the resort made her nervous. Surely someone would notice they weren't a real couple? Maybe if they kept their heads down and stayed to themselves they could pull it off.

The cab drove slowly past lush tropical plants. Vibrant greens, pinks, purples and reds. Up ahead she saw the coral-colored stucco of the main hotel. Beyond that, the pristine white sand beach stretched out to meet the aqua-blue sea.

They stopped under a covered portico, and Sarah recognized two of the other contestant couples piling out of cabs in front of hers. They walked toward a path on the side of the resort. Sarah took her time collecting her luggage and paying the cab fare before following them at a distance safe enough to discourage conversation.

The humid air clung to her as she dragged her suitcase down the stone path. She paused every so often to wrench her suitcase back on course. The clack-clackity-clack of the lopsided wheels mixed with the buzz of insects. The path was lined with colorful flowers and shaded by tall palm trees, and the floral scent of hibiscus and jasmine mingled with the salty tang of the ocean.

As she neared the beach, the path opened up to reveal a vast courtyard with scattered seating areas. Stone benches and huge cushioned sectionals were grouped together in conversation areas. Rope hammocks swung lazily between palm trunks. Further into the trees, love seats were hidden away in intimate settings. The entire area was punctuated with five-foot-tall terra-cotta pots massed with colorful flowers exploding from the top and lush vines trailing down the sides.

Set back from the courtyard, and located on the sugar-white sands of the beach, were ten tropical-style bungalows. They were scattered so that each one was offset from the other for privacy. Each featured a small deck at the front.

Discreet arrow-shaped, knee-high signposts made of teak provided directions toward each bungalow. The one she would share with Raffe was bungalow eight, and a flurry of nerves beat against her rib cage as she realized she was almost there. Her whole body tensed, the edge of the plastic key card she'd been given by one of the contest staff members dug into her sweaty palm. What in the world was she getting herself into?

Walking onto the small wooden deck, she fumbled with the card, jostling her purse, the contents almost spilling onto the deck. She lunged to retrieve it as Raffe opened the door.

"Come on in," he said cheerfully, gesturing with his hand like a maitre'd inviting her into a fine restaurant. Or was it like a spider inviting a fly into his web? Marly had claimed Raffe was a gentleman, but Sarah couldn't be entirely sure what he was thinking now that they had to live together.

The bungalow was light and airy. An open concept with a large living room featuring double sliding glass doors revealed an expanse of frothy sea-green water beyond the private beach. On the far right, a row of cobalt blue cabanas dotted the beach in front of the main resort.

Raffe had opened the sliding doors, and a breeze wafted in, bringing with it a tinge of briny sea air. The cry of gulls punctuated the crashing of surf pounding the beach.

The living room sported a comfy-looking rattan-and-white-linen sofa and two matching chairs. Pillows in bright shades of coral, yellow, and lime green added a splash of color. In front of the couch, a funky, modern coffee table sat low to the floor, and matching side tables held tall lime-green vases, each with a beautiful purple orchid.

To the immediate right was a small kitchen with a granite breakfast bar and two stools. It was decent sized, maybe even bigger than the one in her dinky apartment back in New York.

"Wow, this place is great!" Sarah dragged her suitcase past the kitchen to a short hallway with a door on either side. The one on the right led to a lavishly appointed bathroom with a walk-in shower and modern aqua-glass bowl sinks. The entire room was done in soothing sand-colored matte tile. Accents and towels in aqua and blue added a tropical vibe.

Opposite the bathroom was the bedroom, at the heart of which sat a king-sized four-poster bed, strewn with rose petals in the shape of a heart.

Jeez, this was something out of a cheesy romance novel.

Marly will love this.

She laughed as she stood at the foot of the bed to snap a few photos for her friend.

"What's so funny?" Raffe stepped into the bedroom just as Sarah was making a goofy pose and pointing to the rose petals for a selfie to send to Marly.

Shit! Sarah jerked the phone away and straightened, her cheeks heating with embarrassment.

"Oh. Uh. Umm. Nothing. It's just, I mean the rose petals are funny. Not that they aren't nice, it's just, given our situation, they are kind of funny."

"Oh, yeah, I guess. Anyway, I already assumed I'll sleep on the couch." Raffe said, pointing toward the living room. "By the way, the rose petals were already there when I came in."

Sarah's cheeks burned even hotter. Did Raffe think

that she thought *he* had put them on the bed and she was taking the photo to show off?

"Oh, okay. Thanks. So I guess we should put our stuff away before we head to the meet and greet?" She swept a bunch of the rose petals aside, their sweet floral scent wafting up as they floated to the ground. She hefted her suitcase onto the bed.

The meet-and-greet party was scheduled to begin soon in the courtyard so the contestants could get to know each other. Sarah was anxious about going to the party, but she knew that trying to get out of it would only call attention to her and Raffe. They didn't need any added scrutiny.

She worried about being able to pull off their fake engagement, but going to the party did have a benefit: She wouldn't have to hang around in the bungalow alone with Raffe and the gigantic bed.

"Yeah, there are some drawers in the funky side tables in the living room, and I'll put my clothes in there so I don't have to disrupt you here in the bedroom," Raffe disappeared, and Sarah unzipped her suitcase. She didn't have much in it. Unlike most women, she'd never felt the need to pack a complete wardrobe. She had her chef's clothes, some T-shirts, shorts, a few capri pants, and two dressy outfits. And, of course, flip-flops.

She kicked off her shoes, the tile floor cool on her feet as she padded around the room taking her neatly packed things out of the suitcase and putting them in the drawers. Even though the bedroom was not on the ocean side, she still heard the lulling sound of the surf through the open window. The muted-green and sky-blue tones of the bedroom were soothing, and the king-sized bed, with its fluffy, crisp, white comforter, looked inviting. No time to nap now, though.

UNZIPPING the side pocket of the suitcase, she pulled out her toothbrush, shampoo, soap, and a small makeup case. Sarah had been a tomboy growing up and had never really gotten into the whole makeup and beauty regimen. She'd only started wearing makeup when she had gone to work at Draconia Fashions before her chef job a few years ago, and even then it was only some light bronzer with the occasional dab of lip gloss.

MAYBE SHE SHOULD PUT in a little more effort for this party tonight?

SHE UNZIPPED HER MAKEUP CASE, taking inventory as she crossed the hall to the bathroom. Mascara. Lip gloss. Should she have brought eyeliner?

Ooof! She smacked into something solid. Raffe.

"Sorry, I wasn't looking where I was going." Raffe laughed as they jostled around each other in the doorway.

Sarah squeezed past him into the bathroom.

"Is that all yours?" Sarah pointed to the miscellaneous products neatly tucked onto one side of the large marble vanity. Various skin creams and hair care items. Though Raffe had chopped off his long hair for the contest, he had more personal care items than a girl. Certainly more than she did.

"Yeah," Raffe mumbled, his face reddening. "Hey, guys need to look good too."

"I know, I know. I'm just feeling foolish because you have more than me!" Sarah winced as his cheeks grew more crimson. His usual arrogance was gone, and she almost felt uncomfortable for him, but his embarrassment made her like him a little bit more. It made him more human.

"Umm, do you mind if I hang my suits in the bedroom closet?" Raffe shot over his shoulder as he headed toward the living room.

"Of course not," Sarah said. "Use the bureaus too if you want. I only need two drawers."

"I'm good." Raffe came down the hall with a charcoal-gray suit on a hanger as Sarah headed back into the bedroom. That reminded her, she had a few nice things that should probably be hung up. She grabbed them out of the drawer and snagged a hanger, trying not to brush against Raffe, who was fiddling with his suits, apparently making sure they wouldn't wrinkle on the hanger.

"I feel bad," Sarah blurted out, shutting her empty suitcase and pushing it under the bed.

"Why? What's wrong?" he asked as they both headed toward the living room.

"It's just, well, the engaged part. I hate lying to everyone. I mean, I hope I can pull it off. I'm not very good at lying."

Raffe looked out the window, his eyes pensive, jaw tight. Sarah got the impression that lying bothered him as much as it did her. Maybe there was a softer side under Raffe's hardened businessman-who-would-do-anything-to-succeed persona.

"I don't like lying either, but we aren't hurting anyone." His eyes flew to the fake engagement ring that she nervously twisted on her finger. He frowned, and she stopped twisting then looked out at the ocean.

One of the other couples from the show walked by at the water's edge, their sandals in one hand as their feet splashed in the water. They held hands, laughing.

"They must be heading to the party. We'd better go." Sarah turned, the pressure in her chest growing tight. "I hope I can pull this off."

"You'll be fine. Stop playing with your ring, though. That's a dead giveaway. Just act natural, and no one will suspect a thing."

4

Just act natural, and no one will suspect a thing.

Sarah repeated the mantra in her head as she walked next to Raffe along the solar-light-dotted path that led to the party area.

Her stomach knotted. Not only were she and Raffe *not* a couple, she knew little about him and his personal life and vice versa. Should they have concocted some kind of story? What if people asked personal questions?

As they approached the courtyard, she heard the murmur of voices, bursts of laughter, and the clinking of glasses and utensils. The aroma of grilled meat spiced the air. The knot in her stomach tightened further.

Tiki torches lighted the courtyard, their bright flames flickering above the colorful party lights strung around the perimeter. An ice sculpture depicting the Chef Masters logo—a giant knife—rose eight feet high in the center of the courtyard. The sharp point at the top had already melted to a dull arc, and the handle was dripping. Sarah wondered how long the rest of it would last in the tropical heat. Cans of Sterno burbled under food stations set up in a long row, and servers dressed in island attire passed trays of hors d'oeuvres. A calypso band played softly off to one side, adding the perfect Caribbean touch.

She followed Raffe to a tiki bar and ordered an "Island Special"—which a drink menu described as spiced rum and punch. The bartender handed them the tall pink drinks, placing a little umbrella next to the pineapple slice at the top. Sarah took a long sip. Fruity, spicy, and loaded with rum.

"Excuse me, but that looks delicious, what is it?" a cheerful voice next to her asked.

Sarah turned slightly to her right to find a short, tanned bald man with a warm smile. He wore a bright red Hawaiian shirt and khaki shorts. She recognized him from the contest.

"It's an Island Special. It's delicious. I'm Sarah, by the way. And this is my, err, Raffe. My fiancé." She hoped her new friend hadn't noticed her fumble her words. She was sure Raffe had caught it, though, so she avoided looking at him.

"I'm Rob. So nice to meet you! Honey? Here, this is Sarah and Raffe. This is my partner, Brian." Rob gestured toward a tall, slender man with a gray goatee.

Sarah and Raffe shook Brian's hand and exchanged some small talk while picking from the serving trays paraded past them. Brian and Rob were from Florida, had been together for almost ten years, and were very funny. Sarah liked them immediately.

As they talked, they migrated toward the dining tables, Raffe talking to Brian and Rob about some restaurants in the Boca Raton area that they might know.

"I guess we can sit here?" she asked, stopping at a table where several people were already seated.

"Oh, honey, sure. Sit right down," a woman across from her said. "Make some room, everyone!" she bellowed down toward the end of the table. At the end, a dark-haired woman rolled her eyes and whispered into what Sarah assumed was her husband's ear.

"I'm Gina, and this is my husband Tony. Nice to meet you." The first woman extended a long tanned arm. Dozens of gold bracelets clanked on her wrist as they shook hands.

"That's Kim and her hubby Dave, and down there are Brenda and Dick, and across from them are Tom and Kelly."

Everyone at the table eyed Sarah and Raffe expectantly, so she made the introductions, careful not to stumble over the word "fiancé" when she introduced Raffe.

"Fiancé? I thought this contest was just for married folks," Brenda, the eye roller, said. Sarah sensed trouble and avoided answering her, instead sitting in the chair Raffe had pulled out for her next to Kim. Brian and Rob had already taken seats at the other end of the table.

"How long have you been engaged? Your ring is so pretty!" Kim asked Sarah, eyeing her diamond.

Sarah twisted the ring, stopping immediately upon catching a glare from Raffe, who sat across the table from her.

"Oh, thank you. We've been engaged for, umm, almost two years now. So many things to do, planning a wedding. You know how it is, I'm sure!" Sarah took another sip of her drink to stop herself from babbling.

Kim laughed. She had a soft, gentle way about her and was very dainty. Her straight, waist-length dirty-blond hair was pulled into a ponytail, and she wore a simple lavender ankle-length tank-style dress.

"She's laughing because we eloped," Dave explained, reaching for the bread basket. "Actually, we got married on this same beach, down more toward the town, though."

"Really? How exciting!" Sarah said, perking up. She'd always thought she wanted a destination wedding. When the time came, of course. Okay, if it came. But hey, she was fake engaged, so why not think about fake wedding plans?

"Well, not exactly exciting. It's kind of a long story. We eloped. We had lived in the community for more than a year and loved it here. We knew we wanted to be together, so we just grabbed a JP and got married on the beach."

"What community? You mean you have a house here,

on the island?" Raffe asked, grabbing the butter and slathering it on a roll.

"We've lived here for a while, yes." Dave looked down at his plate. "Not in a house, though. Not anymore. Long story, but we're kind of between homes right now."

Kim put her hand on Dave's arm. "What Dave means is we're homeless. It wasn't always that way, but we've had a run of bad luck."

Homeless? Sarah's ears perked up at the word. Suddenly she was very interested in what Kim and Dave had to say. Apparently so was everyone else, because the table fell silent as everyone looked at Dave.

"Well, it's such a beautiful island," Sarah said, wanting to break the uncomfortable silence without making Dave and Kim feel bad but having no idea what to say. How did a homeless couple even get on the show?

"I feel I should explain." Dave squeezed Kim's hand. Homeless or not, they seemed extremely happy.

"Kim and I met in Boston five years ago. We've been inseparable ever since. About three years ago I had a great job offer as head chef at L'Ellsipa here on the island. So of course I said yes and insisted Kim quit her job and come with me. Long story short, things didn't work out at L'Ellsipa. It all happened very fast, and before we knew it, we were homeless. We had a small amount of money to get by, and we assumed that finding jobs here would be easier than it was. At first we rented a one-room unit. We eventually ended up living on the beach by the bridge."

Sarah knew exactly where he was talking about. On the cab ride from the airport, the driver had pointed out different points of interest, and she distinctly remembered him saying to avoid the beach area around the bridge as it was known as "Tent City," where the homeless lived.

"I hope this doesn't make anyone uncomfortable." Kim glanced around the table.

"How does a homeless couple even get on the show?" Brenda chimed in, asking the question that Sarah—and probably everyone else—was too polite to ask but wanted to know.

"We heard about it from friends. Word still travels, even in the homeless world. I still know people from when I ran the kitchen at L'Ellsipa," Dave explained. "Anyway, we applied and got accepted. They don't really care where you live."

"He is an amazing chef," Kim added, grinning at her husband.

The servers interrupted the conversation, placing white oval platters of food in the middle of the table. Kalua pork, grilled lamb, steak kabobs, grilled pineapple, spiced rice, chicken, and in the middle, a tropical green salad with fruit and nuts.

"So, are there a lot of homeless people on the island?" Sarah tried to sound casual as she reached for the grilled lamb.

"Why would you ask that?" Brenda snapped at her.

"Oh, sorry. I didn't mean to offend anyone," Sarah

stuttered. "It's just that... umm... there's just so much extra food that gets tossed in the contest. I would love to see it go to people who can use it instead of it being thrown away." It was true, except that wasn't *exactly* the reason she'd asked.

Dave smiled. "No worries. There are a lot of homeless. And it's nice of you to think about feeding them. Most of the homeless are just regular folks who had some bad luck like us. But if you have to be homeless, this isn't such a bad place."

"I guess not." Sarah focused on loading up her dish from the platters.

"Raffe, your name is so unique. Is it a family name?" Gina, who sat next to Raffe, leaned in closer to him.

"Thank you. No, not a family name. My parents just liked to be different I guess," Raffe replied, looking almost embarrassed.

Was Gina flirting with him?

Sarah shot a look across the table at Gina, who was staring up at Raffe. She darted her eyes to Raffe. Was he blushing?

She looked back at Gina. She had an unnatural-looking tan, most likely from a tanning bed. Her face was pretty, but too made up. She wore pink lipstick that made her face look almost orange. Sort of like an Oompa Loompa.

"Well, it suits you. It's such a strong name," Gina's eyes lingered on Raffe for a few seconds before returning to her plate.

Well, this was awkward. How was Sarah supposed to feel about someone flirting with her fake fiancé? Should she have fake jealousy? What did Gina's husband, Tony, think of it? He seemed oblivious, focusing on a conversation about sports at the other end of the table.

Sarah concentrated on her meal. She didn't want to get involved with any of these people. If Raffe wanted to do some extra-credit cooking with Gina, then he was more than welcome. As long as it didn't jeopardize their chances of winning, she didn't care what he did.

Sarah focused on making small talk, and before she knew it, they were digging into the crème brûlée. The party was almost over. It hadn't been as bad as she'd thought. No one had asked much about their relationship, and Sarah had been surprised at how easily she could fake the answers to the questions they did ask.

"So what do you guys say? One last drink?" Raffe looked at the others expectantly as he pushed up from the table.

"Sure!" Tony got up too. "I'll get them with you."

The two men went to the bar and came back with tall, umbrella-laced drinks for everyone.

"A toast to good cooking!" Dave held his glass up, and they all reached over the table to clink.

Landon Barkley appeared at the head of the table, beaming smiles at them. "Wonderful! I see you are all getting along nicely. Maybe even making friends, right?" He raised his brows and looked at everyone.

"Yeah!"

"Sure!"

Landon's eyes narrowed like a hawk looking at a baby rabbit. "Great, but I must warn you all not to get too attached. This *is* a contest, after all. And tomorrow one couple will be going home."

The party had gone better than Raffe had expected. A few times he'd seen Sarah twisting that ring and worried she'd blurt something out and give them away, but she'd performed well. Still, he was glad it was over and they were now standing in front of their bungalow. Felt weird, though, coming home to a romantic bungalow with someone he barely knew.

He opened the door and gestured for Sarah to go in first. "After you."

His phone rang before he could enter. It was his best friend, Jasper. He sat on the deck, kicking his expensive leather boat shoes off and sticking his feet into the still-warm sand.

"How's island life?" Jasper asked.

"Better than where you are, I'm sure." Raffe grinned as he dug his toes in deeper, listening to the soothing sound of the surf and feeling the warm breeze on his face. The weather on the island was nearly perfect, but Jasper was in New York, where it was cold and snowy.

"You can say that again. We just got more than a foot of snow. That's why I'm calling. To see if you needed me to check on EightyEight for you?"

Raffe's heart warmed at Jasper's offer. EightyEight was Raffe's soon-to-be-opened restaurant in New York City. Renovations were still underway, behind schedule due to the rough winter. This storm had probably stalled construction even further, and while Raffe had a general manager to look after the project, there was nothing like a friend looking in on your interests for you.

"If you could check it out, I'd appreciate it. Thanks. Anything new?" Raffe asked.

"Aside from Edward driving me nuts? Nothing. For a retired person, he works more now than before." Jasper's voice held a lilt of exasperation when he mentioned his father.

The two could not get along. Raffe, on the other hand, got along with Edward just fine. Having known him since he was in grade school, Raffe considered him a second father of sorts, one that had paid more attention to him than his own father. But Edward didn't hold Raffe to the impossibly high standards he held Jasper to, and that made for an easier relationship.

Edward had a rough exterior, but he also had a huge heart and was an honorable man. Raffe thought the world of him, and he knew that the only reason he was so hard on Jasper was because he loved his son deeply.

"Maybe you should have Edward keep an eye on EightyEight for me. That oughtta keep him busy." Raffe smirked. Edward was a bulldog when it came to business. He would drive Raffe's general manager crazy at EightyEight, but that was okay. He trusted Edward, and knew he'd make sure the project was going smoothly.

"Great idea. That will keep him out of my hair too." Jasper paused for a second. "So, how's the engagement going?"

Raffe heard the tone of humor creep into his friend's voice. Ever since Jasper had become engaged, it seemed he'd made it his hobby to make sure Raffe suffered the same fate.

"Dude, it's fake. Nothing's going on. Sarah's a nice girl, but it's just for the contest," Raffe said. Jasper was one of the few people who knew the engagement was phony. It had been his fianceé Marly's idea, and Jasper had encouraged it. But if he thought it would turn into something more, he was wrong. Sarah was nice, but he didn't want to get involved with her romantically. His romances always blew up, and because she was a good friend of theirs, it was best to keep things purely platonic.

"Well, you never know what might happen," Jasper sounded hopeful. The guy just wouldn't give up.

"The show's going good so far. I'll keep you updated. Tell your *real* fiancé I said hi." Raffe disconnected and stepped into the bungalow.

Sarah sat at the kitchen counter texting. She'd taken

her hair out of the bun she'd worn to the party, and it flowed down her back, shimmering like corn silk.

Raffe glanced at the couch. Should he pull out the sleeper bed? What about pajamas? He certainly couldn't walk around in his boxers as he did at home.

He grabbed some cotton striped pajama bottoms and a T-shirt from the side table drawer then made his way into the bathroom while Sarah was still occupied, eager to avoid an awkward encounter if they both wanted to use it at the same time. He changed in record time and splashed some cold water on his face, drying it off with one of the fluffy hand towels neatly stacked on the vanity.

"Marly sends her best," Sarah said as he emerged from the bathroom. She hopped off the stool and moved to the sofa. Raffe started toward the sofa to join her but instead opted to sit on the chair. Now that the two of them were alone in the bungalow for the rest of the night, he felt awkward.

"How is she?" he asked.

"She's great. Still going in a million directions planning the wedding. Of course, Edward wants it to be a huge event, and Jasper and Marly just want it over with. Oh, and she's planning it all around Fall Fashion Week because she can't miss that."

Raffe grinned, happy that Marly's plus-size line had been such a huge success for Jasper's company, Draconia Fashions. Jasper had met his match. Raffe had never seen him as happy as he was with Marly. Apparently the right woman really could change your life.

"So, what did you think about our competition?" Raffe genuinely wanted to know Sarah's opinion of the other contestants.

"Hmm. Well, they are all interesting, that's for sure. Kim and Dave seem so down to earth. I liked them the most."

"Yeah, they seemed nice. They really laid it all on the line to get into this contest, but even though they're facing tough times they still seem really happy, almost carefree." Raffe felt a pang of guilt bordering on jealousy. Dave and Kim had worked hard and earned a spot on the show while Raffe had lied to get his way in.

"I know. It puts things in perspective, right?" Sarah sighed. "But then there was Brenda. She was the complete opposite."

"Yeah, she was a loudmouth," Raffe said.

"I guess there's one in every group. She seems like she could be trouble. And Gina seems a little flirty." Sarah glanced at him out of the corner of her eye. Raffe wondered what she was getting at. He'd noticed Gina had paid some attention to him, but Raffe was used to that. He didn't think she had been flirting. Was she?

"Gina's harmless. She's got her husband, anyway, and he seems a handful."

"I wonder if any of them stole our walnuts and our eggs," Sarah said.

"I don't think so. I mean, why would they single us

out? It's possible that it was a part of the challenge. Or a mistake." Did Sarah really think someone had tried to sabotage them? Raffe doubted any of the contestants would have had time to take the eggs or the walnuts. How could they when they were busy in their own kitchens? And besides, it was against contest rules to go into another team's kitchen area.

"Well, of all the teams, you have the most overall experience. I mean, you own five-star restaurants, so someone might have wanted to make sure you had a disadvantage."

"True, but I'm still not convinced that someone tried to sabotage us. It was probably just a mistake."

Sarah was quiet, staring out the sliding glass door at the ocean, where sparkles of moonlight danced on the waves. Despite the beautiful scene in front of them, her mouth was drawn in a tight line. "I hope you're right, but something tells me those missing ingredients were no mistake."

TJ PUNCHED out on the old time clock, looking over the hours he'd accumulated for the week. He'd been working a lot of overtime due to the amount of extra cookware the show constantly required, and the money was adding up. Good. The more he made, the sooner he could really get his life on track.

He exited by the side door that led to the less-traveled

alley beside the conference center. TJ always liked to take the less-traveled route. The fewer people he came in contact with, the better.

He'd resisted making friends, keeping to himself and paying little attention to the workplace scuttlebutt. He didn't even really know much about the cooking show. He didn't know the names of the contestants or the names of his coworkers.

The job was just temporary, a means to an end, but he was lucky to get it. There weren't many opportunities for someone in his situation. He wasn't here to make friends. His goal was to remain nearly invisible. It was better for everyone that way.

His worn sneakers crunched on the path of crushed shells, the sole flapping where it parted from the rest of the shoe as he made his way toward the edge of the property.

As he passed the end of the building, the scent of roasted meat caught his attention. He'd heard the crazy blonde yelling about making sure they had enough chafing dishes available for some party in the courtyard, and he knew the night cleaning crew wouldn't sweep through for another twenty minutes.

Would there be any leftover food in the courtyard? He veered toward the beach, not on the path—he didn't want to be seen—but through the trees. He pushed past shrubs and scrubby palms, the leaves slapping his arms as he tried to avoid stepping on any flowers or smaller plants. A small animal scurried out of his way just as he came upon the courtyard.

The delicious smell grew stronger as he got closer. He stood back in the shadows to make sure no one was still milling about. His stomach grumbled, a reminder that he hadn't eaten since lunch.

The courtyard was empty, the tables strewn with a few empty glasses from partygoers who had lingered longer than the serving crew. Plates and chafing dishes were piled in the area behind the tiki hut they used as a bar for events like this. The serving crew had cleared the tables and left the majority of dishes and glasses behind the tiki bar for the night crew.

There was a puddle in the middle of the courtyard, as if something big had melted. TJ glanced up at the cameras hidden in the tops of the palm trees to see if the red lights were on, but they were all off.

He walked over to the chafing dishes, which were still warm, and grabbed a piece of the Kalua pork, his stomach cramping almost as soon as he swallowed it. The sweet, savory taste was much richer than anything he was used to eating.

Golden rolls were piled in a basket beside the chafing dish. He stuffed his pockets full. What a shame the show wasted so much food. TJ knew dozens of starving people. At least he could take them the rolls.

Something made a scraping sound on the stone walkway, and he froze. An animal? No, it sounded like a person approaching. Panic shot through him, and he jumped away from the food, turning quickly and disappearing into the foliage.

VERONICA WATCHED the food-stealing dishwasher disappear. What had he been doing out here? She debated calling out to stop him, but then she'd have to lecture him and that would just take time. Besides, it was her job to make sure that everything was cleaned up, and that hadn't even been done yet. Now she would have to go yell at the kitchen staff again.

She was exhausted from the stupid party the show's producers had insisted she set up so that the contestants could "mingle." She had run around behind the scenes during the party and had no energy to argue with this fool over why he was stealing rolls.

She sank into one of the chairs. It was soft and comfortable, much nicer than anything near the low-end part of the resort where her room was.

She toed off her plain white sandals and rubbed her aching feet, leaning her head back to look up at the stars. She could see so many of them down here, much more than in New York City. Thoughts of the city sent a pang of homesickness through her. No sense in dwelling on that now. She had a job to do here.

She shoved her feet back into her sandals. They weren't the nicest shoes she had; that pair had two-inch rhinestone-studded heels. But she couldn't wear those anymore. They hurt her feet. Besides, heels weren't practical for a job that demanded you run around all day.

She glanced around the area, eyeing the large wet spot where the ice sculpture had stood. She'd better make sure one of the night crew mopped that up. She didn't want one of the contestants to slip on it and sue the resort. Somehow that would end up being her fault.

She pushed up from the chair. Good thing the cameras were off, because the producers would have a fit if they saw her sitting here. You could see everything on those cameras. She knew that because just a few hours ago she'd been sitting in the control room watching images of Raffe and Sarah. She'd been able to watch and listen in on their super boring conversations via all the monitors and microphones.

What a dull group of people. Especially Sarah! Why had she gone on and on about the homeless people on this island? Who cared?! Veronica wondered if anyone would even want to watch the show if this was what they'd air between the actual cooking contests.

She walked slowly back to the conference center. She'd been heading to her room, but now she had to double back to make sure the night crew was going to come and clean up. As she walked she made a mental note to annoy the dishwasher again tomorrow. For some reason she liked to stress him out.

Raffe rearranged his knives on the cutting board for the third time. The overhead lights glinted off the blades, the smooth wooden handles and heft of the expensive chef's knives were comforting in his hand. He needed comfort. Waiting for Landon Barkley to announce their next contest had his nerves on edge.

That morning in the bungalow hadn't been as awkward as he'd thought. He and Sarah had gotten along easily, sipping coffee and packing their knives for the challenge. But when they'd arrived at the conference center, all the couples had been separated, and Sarah had gone off to a kitchen in another part of the center. For what, Raffe didn't know, but whatever it was couldn't be good.

A fist of doubt squeezed his heart. Sarah was the one who thought quickly on her feet. Would he be able to pull off a challenge without her?

"Attention, chefs! I hope you are enjoying your time here and your private bungalows. Perhaps it has brought some of our couples even closer." Landon paused with a sappy smile on his face and looked around the room. "And you'll thank me for that in this next challenge."

The other chefs shuffled their feet uneasily.

"This contest will determine how well you really know your significant other."

Raffe's head jerked up to see Landon with a wicked gleam in his eye.

Shit!

"You are to recreate your partner's favorite meal, dessert included." Landon gestured toward two staff members who were handing out index cards. "Fill out the cards in front of you with your favorite meal. Your significant other will be doing the same in our duplicate kitchens on the other side of the conference center. I hope you've been paying attention to what your loved one likes to eat. You will have one hour. Time starts... *now!*"

Raffe's stomach sank. He stared at the index card in front of him, racking his brain for what Sarah might think was his favorite meal. Had they ever even eaten together? *His* favorite meal didn't matter, though. He needed to think about Sarah's favorite meal, because that's what he'd have to cook. Why hadn't they gone over basic stuff like this before the show had started?

The other contestants were already rushing to the pantry, grabbing ingredients and stacking them on their counters. He heard the clicking of the gas stove burners lighting and the whir of blenders.

Landon yelled out, "Fifty-five minutes!"

Five minutes had already passed? He'd better get going.

Raffe closed his eyes and tried to think. He'd never really eaten with Sarah other than a few times when she'd been visiting Marly at Jasper's and he'd happened over. But those few times Sarah had been the cook. She'd never talked about her favorite meals, and Raffe assumed she'd been making *Jasper's* favorites because she'd been his assistant.

He opened his eyes, the blank index card staring up at him. Right. Not only did he have to figure out Sarah's favorite meal, he had to try to figure out what Sarah thought *his* favorite was and write it on the card.

Wait. Sarah was in the same boat. She'd be thinking along the same lines. Would she remember the meals from Jasper's and write one down?

One had been an amazing lobster risotto. Raffe had had seconds as well as raved about the meal to Sarah. He might have even asked her for the recipe for one of his chefs. He jotted that down on the card. Next up was dessert. This one was easy, lemon meringue pie. Sarah had made one once that was the best he'd ever had. He had asked Jasper as a joke to make sure she kept all of his fridges stocked with it. He was sure she'd remember that.

But what to make as Sarah's favorite? He had no idea.

Did she like meat or fish? Was she a vegetarian? Food allergies?

She ate a lot of granola bars. That's all he remembered from when she worked for Jasper. Granola and fruit. In fact, aside from last night, he hadn't even seen her eat anything since they'd been on this trip.

What do women like to eat? Salads. That's what all the women he usually dated ate. So boring! Sarah wasn't anything like them.

Okay, the opposite of a salad... meat. What kind of meat? That's it—Sarah liked pork, she had mentioned it at last night's party. He grabbed a cut of pork chops and sweet potatoes as well as ingredients for a rich chocolate mousse for dessert. Every woman loved chocolate, right?

Back at the prep table he scrubbed the potatoes and placed them in the oven then set the chops in a marinade.

"Forty-five minutes!" Raffe jumped as Landon bellowed.

His gut churned. Was he wrong? Maybe she hated chocolate. It was too late now. A wave of longing washed over him. In the first challenge having Sarah in the kitchen beside him had given him a boost of confidence. What if he made an amazing meal but it was the wrong one?

Shaking off his insecurities, he whipped up the chocolate mousse and rushed it over to the large walk-in cooler so it could chill while he worked on the entree.

While they'd been filling out their cards, the cooler had been pre-staged with silver domed platters, each with the contestant's names on them. He found Sarah's and put the mousse under the dome before rushing back to finish the rest of the meal.

VERONICA SLITHERED out from behind her desk, grabbed a large notebook, and headed toward the walk-in coolers, glancing behind her to ensure no one watched. It didn't really matter if anyone did. Her job required her to be all over the set. She was responsible for keeping the production on time, which meant she was basically a glorified babysitter.

A blast of cold air sent goosebumps up her arm as she opened the heavy door of the walk-in. She slipped inside, her eyes darting over the domed platters, stopping at Sarah's.

She lifted the dome, made a fast switch, and hurried out, making a beeline for the storage closet down the hallway, the chocolate mousse clutched to her chest with the notebook held in front to cover it just in case someone came down the usually deserted hall.

Once safely inside, she leaned her back against the door, removed the spoon she had stuffed inside her pocket, and dug into the thick, decadent mousse. She closed her eyes and swirled the creamy dessert around her tongue.

"What are you doing?"

Veronica's heart lurched at the crackly disembodied voice coming from the dark recesses of the room.

"Who the hell are you? And *what* are you doing in here?" Veronica shot back.

The voice didn't answer. Instead she heard a squeaky mechanical whirring.

A figure emerged from the dark corner, gliding out slowly. An older woman in a wheelchair. Veronica pegged her to be in her late sixties or early seventies, and although she hunched over in the chair, she was perhaps one of the most beautiful women Veronica had ever seen.

Her long silver hair was piled into a loose bun on her head. A pale blue-and-green shawl draped loosely around her thin shoulders. Her emerald eyes were striking in both intensity and color, especially given the contrast with her olive skin. Veronica couldn't stop staring at her.

"I'm Gertie O'Rourke."

"You? You're Gertie O'Rourke?" Veronica was dumbfounded. She'd heard the name many times since joining the show and had pictured a young powerhouse, not some old lady in a wheelchair.

Gertie O'Rourke was the executive producer of the show. She called most of the shots. Her name was well known within the cooking industry, something Veronica only discovered through her job. Most people spoke as if they were afraid of her, which intrigued Veronica. She knew Gertie didn't put up with any crap, and she liked that.

"Heh. Not what you expected, huh? Not a lot of people want to see a chef in one of these," Gertie explained, her long fingers gesturing to her wheelchair. "'Course, these days maybe that's changed."

Veronica twisted her lips. Had things changed? Maybe not so much. When the producers were choosing the original chefs to be in the first elimination rounds, they'd veered toward the more attractive contestants. She'd even overheard them saying that prettier faces made for higher ratings. "I'm not so sure things have changed. They seem to be obsessed with good looks in the TV industry." Veronica glanced down at her own body, now three sizes larger than it had been just a few months ago.

Gertie snorted. "Yeah. Always about the looks, isn't it?"

"It usually is." Veronica took another spoonful of the mousse. Her whole life had been about looks. About her being fat. The kids teasing her because of it. Her mother lecturing her. Her father leaving.

But she'd worked hard to overcome that. She'd lost more than one hundred pounds and spin cycled her way down to a size two. That's when she'd gotten the job at Draconia Fashions. Her future had seemed bright. She'd even had a shot at marrying her billionaire boss, Jasper Kenney.

But Sarah and Marly had ruined that. Her brows dipped in an angry scowl as thoughts of how the two women had destroyed her future reminded her of the real reason she took this stupid job.

"I WANTED to be a star chef, you know," Gertie said wistfully.

"Yeah, well welcome to the you-don't-always-get-what-you-want club. I used to want things too."

Gertie eyed her thoughtfully, and Veronica felt the tug of a strange bond forming. She supposed they must have fought similar battles—Gertie with her disability and Veronica with her weight—and Veronica had never met anyone who could commiserate with her. Everyone she knew had led charmed lives compared to hers.

"Back when I started years ago people in wheelchairs weren't as accepted. A TV show with a chef in a wheel-chair? No way was that going to happen. Cooking shows were still new, heck TV was even pretty new. But I wanted to be a pioneer in the culinary television indus-try, so I had no choice but to work behind the scenes. I had to fight to even be able to do that." Gertie's face pinched. "My parents told me I wouldn't do anything with my life, actually that I *couldn't*, because I was disabled. I've been using this godawful contraption since I was two years old, you know."

Veronica stared incredulously at Gertie. She knew *exactly* how the old woman felt. The sudden urge to confide in Gertie made words rush out of her mouth unchecked.

"My parents said the same things about me. I was overweight, and that was my disability. According to them, at least. My father left when I was only five, and my mother always told me it was because I was fat. That I was lazy and obese, and that's what made him leave. And that's why I had no friends or boyfriends..." Veronica's voice trailed off as she tried to push down the painful memories. Like the one about her senior prom, when she'd saved all year to buy the most beautiful plus-sized gown. She could still remember the painful hollow feeling when it became obvious her date wasn't going to show and the twist of the knife in her heart when her mother laughed at her as she stood crying in the doorway.

"That's terrible," Gertie said. "Parents can be cruel, even when they think they are protecting you."

Had her mother been protecting her? Veronica didn't think so. "I tried to lose weight. I tried so hard! The kids at school were so terrible to me. Calling me blubber. It was horrible. I'd come home from school crying, and my mother would tell me that the kids were right, that I was a fat loser."

Veronica's eyes stung. She'd never told anyone this before, but now that it was out she felt a huge relief. Like something malignant had been bottled up inside her festering all these years and she'd just released it.

For a minute she almost felt a little less angry. A little less vindictive. A little less determined to make the world pay. But then suspicion set in. What was this old bat up to anyway, and why the hell had she opened up to her? She didn't even know her.

"Ha! I know just how you feel. Kids were mean to me too. Sometimes they would throw things on the floor so I couldn't get by and my wheels would get stuck. And my parents always seemed angry with me, as though it was my fault. I was so bitter and angry. But I took that anger and turned it into passion. I had always wanted to cook and had spent hours reading cookbooks as well as cooking at my school, thanks to an amazing home economics teacher.

"I wanted my own show, but no one wanted a chef in a wheelchair. So I became the brains behind the first cooking show to ever be televised, and I grew from there. Julia Child and all that wine? My idea. That southern gal who uses all the butter? Also my idea. The tall man who eats bugs and travels to all those exotic places? Yup, that's my idea too. You see, my brainchild was the notion that every chef has to have some kind of gimmick."

Veronica stood silent as she listened, nodding her head. She and Gertie were kindred spirits. It was impressive that Gertie had achieved all that given her disability, especially decades ago. She must have had to overcome a lot. The woman had a will of iron, something Veronica admired. Gertie's pride in her accomplishments was evident the way her face lighted as she told the story. What accomplishments did Veronica have to be proud of?

"You know, I was so angry at the beginning of my

career. I did some mean things and hurt people…" Gertie cocked her head and looked up at Veronica. "Just as I suspect you might be doing. I had that same sour look on my face. But I knew what I was doing was wrong, and I never really felt any satisfaction from being so mean. So, I channeled that negativity into positivity. And you know what? My career really took off after I made that change. And it's been an amazing experience for me ever since. Maybe, if you did the same, your life would be better, you'd be happier."

Gertie's eyes drifted to the chocolate mousse Veronica held, and then she slowly wheeled out of the room, the annoying squeaking of her wheels fading as she moved farther away.

Veronica looked down at the mousse. She had no appetite for it now. That stupid old bat had ruined it with her speech. Yeah, sure she'd overcome a lot of adversity. And sure, she might have seen right through Veronica, but who was she to give a lecture? It reminded Veronica of her mother's lectures.

Landon's voice suddenly filled the air, announcing that time was up. Veronica threw the mousse in the trash and hurried off to watch Raffe and Sarah lose.

SARAH FINISHED PLACING the silver dome over her dish just as Landon yelled out that time was up. She had hustled the entire hour, making sure everything was perfect while worry gnawed at her gut with the doubt that she was even cooking the right dishes.

She'd decided on lobster risotto, because Raffe had raved about it that time at Jasper's. He'd even asked for the recipe, so it seemed a safe bet. She didn't know anything about what the guy liked to eat. Hopefully he'd remember that one meal and be smart enough to figure it was Sarah's only clue to his culinary preferences.

But what did Raffe make for her? He was clueless about what she liked, so she'd tried to put herself in his head and figure out what he might *think* was her favorite.

Men didn't use the same logic, so instead of writing down her actual favorite meal—lasagna—she wrote down something she knew *he* liked—pork. The night before, Raffe had raved about the pork served in the courtyard. And didn't men usually just assume women liked what *they* did when it came to certain things?

That's how Harley, her ex-boyfriend, had been. Every gift he had given her was something that *he* would have liked. They watched the TV shows *he* liked. Lucky thing she wasn't involved with him anymore. He had caused enough damage in her life. Now she got to watch whatever she wanted.

She glanced over at the table that held the finished meals, all sitting under their silver domes. For dessert, she'd made lemon meringue pie. She knew Raffe liked that because he had asked Jasper to keep his fridge stocked with it at one point.

"Time for everyone to join their partner for the

reveals!" Landon barked, herding them all into the adjoining main room as a crew member rushed ahead of them, pushing a cart carrying all of the meals.

Raffe was already there, standing next to a table that had been set up like something you'd find in a fancy restaurant. White tablecloth, crystal goblets, flickering candles, gleaming cutlery, linen napkins, and of course, the meal he'd prepared sitting under its silver dome. There were five other tables, all similarly readied.

Sarah's chest squeezed. Did the other chefs all know their partners' favorites? If so, and Sarah and Raffe had guessed wrong, they'd be going home today.

The crew member placed Sarah's meal next to Raffe's on the table, moving slowly to ensure nothing slid off the plates or that the domes didn't topple. Sarah shot Raffe a quick smile as she walked to the table. Raffe held out her chair and she sat, then he took the seat opposite.

The room filled with the scraping of chairs as all the couples sat. Then Landon finally walked to the first table, Sarah and Raffe's.

"How well do you really know your partner?" Landon glanced around the room. "One of the mainstays of a good marriage is the little details. So this challenge is important. If chef couples can't remember each other's favorite meal, I hardly think that lends itself to matrimonial bliss."

The audience chuckled, and Landon smiled at his own cleverness. "Today's challenge is a little different.

Each couple will enjoy each other's cooking while the judges are doing their tasting."

Sarah's heart thudded as she stared at the silver domes. Would he just get on with it? They'd divided the meal into the dishes under the domes and separate dishes for the judges as instructed. Sarah knew the combination of flavors, consistency, and seasoning of hers was perfect, but was it the right one?

"Raffe and Sarah, please remove the domes on your main courses." Finally.

Sarah's eyes locked with Raffe. Though he appeared calm, she saw a flicker of uncertainty in his eyes. She grabbed the smooth metal of the dome and lifted. Pork chops! At least they would be partly right. She glanced over at Raffe, who was staring at the lobster risotto, a smile quirking his lips. Had she guessed right?

"Please flip over the cards on your table." Landon instructed in a monotone.

They flipped them over, revealing matching foods with what they had each cooked. He had written lobster risotto! Yes!

"Next, the desserts. Please remove the domes."

Raffe removed his dome, revealing Sarah's perfectly peaked lemon meringue pie. Sarah could tell by his reaction that she had guessed correctly.

Sarah slowly lifted her dome, her heart racing. They were batting one thousand. Did she dare hope...?

She stared at the dessert. The dome slipped from her hand, and she had to fumble to recover it before it clattered to the floor. On the plate sat a hot pink marsh-mallow Peep surrounded by M&Ms.

What the hell kind of dessert was that? And why the hell would Raffe have chosen it? She didn't remember ever mentioning Peeps or M&Ms to him, and aside from being ugly and bizarre, it wasn't even something that required cooking!

She jerked her eyes up to Raffe, who stared down at the ugly dessert, apparently just as dumbfounded.

"Well, that's certainly *different*," Durkin said, emphasizing the word different and not in a positive way. "I didn't realize we stocked Peeps."

Raffe opened his mouth to say something, but all that came out was gibberish. Knowing that the judges wanted an explanation, Sarah swooped in to save them.

"I can't believe he did this! We had our first date the day after Easter, and I had mentioned how I didn't get any candy for Easter. Peeps are my favorite, and when dessert was brought out for us, it was Peeps and M&Ms," Sarah gushed, hoping she sounded believable. What a stupid story! Peeps! Ha! If this had happened in real life, she would not have been impressed, but she smiled and hoped the judges bought her story. It was their only hope, because she sure as hell hadn't written Peeps and M&Ms on the card. She'd written chocolate mousse!

The judges and other contestants all broke into a collective "Awwww."

Unfortunately, it wasn't written on the card. Landon took glee in telling them that even though the story was cute, it was points off for the mismatch. Sarah was just happy they hadn't been laughed out of the contest. What had Raffe been thinking?

The only saving grace was that they scored high points on the judges' tasting. Landon went down the row, revealing each of the other couples' meals as Sarah picked at the pork chop in front of her. As he proceeded, her spirits picked up a little. Most of the other couples hadn't guessed correctly either, and some of them lost points on the tasting.

After all the reveals were completed, only one couple got everything correct: Brian and Rob. Sarah and Raffe came in third. Unfortunately, Tom and Kelly came in last and were eliminated. Sarah had mixed feelings. She liked Tom and Kelly, but she didn't want to be the one sent home. Maybe it was better not to like any of the other contestants.

"Ladies and gentlemen, congratulations on your win. To help you celebrate, we have a special treat for you!" Landon bellowed.

A special treat! Last time the treat had been their accommodations. Not such a great thing in Sarah's point of view. So this time it *had* to be something good. Maybe this time it was money or a car. She could certainly use both. Although, on second thought, a car isn't really practical when you live in New York City. Her thoughts were interrupted by Landon's announcement.

"We have flown in two family members for each of

you, and they are waiting for you in your bungalows! Have a great night!"

Family members? What did he mean? Sarah's chest flooded with panic. The only two family members she'd listed on her application were her parents, and that was in case of emergency. The same parents who knew nothing about her fake engagement.

Everyone else cheered; they were all thrilled. Sarah felt the pork chops rising in her throat...

7

F amily members? Raffe doubted any of his would come, but it seemed as if Sarah would have a nice family. So why did she have that look of panic on her face?

Raffe was about to ask her when Gina waltzed over to them and gave Raffe a very long and borderline inappropriate hug.

"Congratulations!" she exclaimed loudly, glancing back at her husband as she squeezed Raffe.

Raffe tensed, his arms at his side, as Gina hugged him tightly. It was a little too tight for his liking. What was going on here? He saw Tony giving him a dirty look out of the corner of his eye. He didn't want to be rude and brush Gina off but at the same time couldn't help but feel that she was being a bit over the top and showboating. Kim and Dave had also won, and she had walked right past them without a word of congratulations.

"We should really get going, Raffe," Sarah gave him a raised brow look and walked away.

He stepped back from Gina's grasp and quickly thanked her then bolted for the door to catch up with Sarah.

"Hey, wait up!" he called. She was already part way down the path that led to the bungalows.

"Oh, sorry. I wasn't sure if you wanted to stay and chat some more with Gina," Sarah smiled at him. Any hint of jealousy that Raffe had thought he'd seen was no longer there. Probably imagined it. Had he wanted Sarah to be jealous?

"What was up with that Peeps dessert, anyway?" She made a face. "Do you realize that could have sent us home?"

Raffe held his hand up. "I had nothing to do with that. I made a chocolate mousse, not that ridiculous Peep and M&M monstrosity. Someone swapped them out. I guess you were right about the eggs and walnuts after all. Someone *is* trying to sabotage us."

"I don't get it." Sarah stopped in her tracks and turned to Raffe, lowering her voice. "All the other chefs seem so nice. Who would play dirty like that?"

Raffe saw she was genuinely perplexed. Sarah wasn't used to the ugly side of business in which most people would screw their grandmother to get ahead. But Raffe was, and the reason was obvious. "There's a lot of money involved. Sometimes that brings out the worst in people."

"Are they doing the same to the other teams? We have to tell Landon."

A lizard darted in front of them, and Raffe watched its speckled body disappear into the plants lining the path. Should they tell Landon? Raffe's killer business instinct told him that might not be a smart move. "Hold on. Whoever it is hasn't succeeded in making us lose so far. Both times we came out fine."

"Yes, but maybe we won't next time," Sarah said.

"I think we need to see if we can get some proof first. It might backfire if we go around accusing someone without proof." Raffe tilted his head. "That was a great save with the Peep story, by the way."

Sarah's face cracked into a proud smile. "Thanks. I'm not usually good at making stuff up, but I was desperate and it popped into my head. Guess we're even after that save you did with the Waldorf salad in the first contest." Sarah started walking again. "You may be right about not telling Landon. Let's keep our eyes open, though."

"Deal. We'll be extra watchful." Raffe stuck his fist out and Sarah bumped it. He felt a rush of warmth. They were in this together.

He had to admit he'd been skeptical at first. He knew Sarah could cook, but he had no idea if they'd get along. Was she one of those domineering, bossy women who would want to take control? Or was she the wimpy type who couldn't make a decision? Turned out she was neither. She was perfectly capable, smart, and a great partner.

Sarah was someone he could trust and rely on. She didn't expect him to carry all the weight. It was a nice change for him to share the pressure with someone instead of taking it all on his shoulders.

Sarah stopped abruptly as they reached the clearing where the path ended and the beach began. The bungalows were twenty feet away.

She looked up at him, worry darkening her amber eyes. "We do have another problem. In about one minute you're going to meet my parents, and I'm going to meet yours. I don't know what you told yours, but mine have no idea about our fake engagement. I'm not sure we can pull this off."

Raffe frowned. "I'm pretty sure it will be only your parents that are there. Mine are overseas, and even if they weren't, I doubt they'd come."

He looked away at the pity that flickered in her eyes. He didn't need anyone's sympathy for his parents' lack of interest in his life. He was used to it. "I'm not that close with my family, but don't worry. It will be fine. We can fake it for a short visit. Besides, I'm a great catch!" He made a goofy face to lighten the mood and was rewarded with her melodic laughter.

"Okay, I guess you're right." Sarah continued toward the bungalow.

Raffe followed, stopping at the door, his hand on the latch. "Ready?"

Sarah hesitated for a second. She smoothed her shirt and fluffed her hair. She darted a look in the direction of the bar, and for a minute Raffe wondered if she was going to run off, but then she took a deep breath and refocused on the bungalow door. "Yep. Here goes nothing!"

Raffe held the door open for Sarah, and she walked inside the bungalow ahead of him.

"Sarah!" both her parents exclaimed in unison. They rushed to her, their happiness evident on their faces.

A stab of envy speared Raffe's heart. Had his parents ever been that happy to see him? Memories of years of summer reunions after attending boarding school surfaced. He couldn't recall his parents ever fawning over him like this. In fact, they usually sent the chauffeur to collect him. Edward Kenney and his now-deceased wife had shown a warmer welcome when Raffe had gone to their house in the Hamptons to visit Jasper than Raffe's own parents.

Once the round of hugging was over, Raffe introduced himself to her parents, who looked to be in their midfifties. They had the contented look of hardworking people, not the polished, bored look of rich people who had been handed everything and still weren't satisfied.

They looked him over critically. Raffe couldn't blame them, given the situation.

"It's a pleasure to meet both of you," Raffe added, looking to Sarah for some help. He hoped to be able to leave it up to her to do most of the talking.

"I'm sure it seems crazy that I'm engaged, but everything happened so fast!" she exclaimed, stepping next to Raffe and putting her arm around him.

Raffe watched her in admiration as she made up a whopping lie as to how they'd met, the brief courtship, and how he had proposed.

She explained not telling them by saying he'd proposed the night before the contest and she hadn't wanted to call and tell them as she'd wanted them both to do it in person. She apologized to them sincerely, saying that, because the contest wouldn't air for a few months, they'd have told them in plenty of time before they saw it on television. She even gushed over the details, just as if they really were engaged. Not too shabby for such a last-minute drill.

"Well, it's wonderful that you're so happy, dear, but that ring, it just, well... it doesn't seem like the type of ring you'd wear, honey." Sarah's mother grabbed Sarah's hand and gawked at the fake diamond ring then slid her eyes over to Raffe.

"I picked the ring out myself," Raffe spoke up, defending his choice of a fake engagement ring. In the real world, he would have asked Sarah's father's permission before proposing.

Maybe that wasn't the right thing to say, judging by the look Sarah shot him.

"Well, if that's the case, you two might want to have a long engagement. You don't know my daughter very well if you think she wants to wear this type of ring on her finger for the rest of her life," Sarah's mother's cutting words were delivered with a genuine smile that diffused the remark. "I'm sure you will learn in time."

Another man might have gotten angry, but Raffe liked Sarah's mother. She was feisty, and he admired that she was looking out for her daughter. Oddly enough, he wanted her to like him, and it seemed like he hadn't made the best impression thus far. Fake fiancé or not, he wanted her to accept him.

"I wanted it to be a surprise, but maybe I should have asked. What kind of ring *would* you like?" Raffe asked, looking down at the somewhat gaudy cubic zirconia on Sarah's finger. He supposed it *was* a bit ostentatious.

"I... I mean I love this one because you picked it out yourself." Sarah shot a look at her mother. "I usually go for more simple jewelry. My grandmother had a small diamond with a sapphire on either side as her wedding ring, and I loved to wear it when I was a little girl. But really, Raffe, I love this ring."

"Oh, it's fine. Besides, it isn't about the ring, it's about how happy our daughter is," Sarah's father, Bruce, chimed in, throwing his wife a disapproving look. "Michelle just likes to put all of Sarah's boyfriends through the ringer!"

They all laughed, and the awkward chill that had pervaded the room was replaced with a strange warm acceptance. He'd passed the first test, apparently.

"Wait, *all* of her boyfriends? How many has she had?" Raffe joked, making them all laugh even more.

Sarah's eyes twinkled as she giggled, and he slid his

arm round her shoulders for effect, surprised at how easy it was for them to act as if they really *were* engaged.

"So, have you heard from Tommy at all? Does he know yet?" Sarah's mother's tone was a little strange, and she looked at Sarah with hopeful eyes before reaching for a grape from the fruit and cheese platter the show had delivered to the bungalow.

Sarah's smile slipped, and she shot a harsh look at her mother. "Let's go sit outside. It's gorgeous on the deck."

Tommy. Hmm… Definitely something odd going on there. Must be her ex-boyfriend. And the mother clearly still likes him. An unreasonable pang of jealousy shot through Raffe.

Smarten up! You aren't really engaged. All this family closeness must be messing with your head. Sarah already had the doors open and was rearranging the chairs on the deck. He was surprised at what a good liar she was. Just like his ex, Lauren. Don't all women eventually lie, though?

Michelle was busy pouring more wine. She hadn't persisted with the Tommy question, but Sarah had made it clear that she didn't want them talking about him.

Raffe grabbed the tray of fruit, crackers, and cheese and walked toward the deck, Sarah's parents in tow with their full wine glasses. They all settled into the cushioned wicker chairs and watched the ocean.

"So, how have the contests gone so far?" Sarah's mother asked as she balanced a piece of cheese on top of a Ritz.

Raffe and Sarah took turns describing what had happened so far in the contest, each playing off the other's words like a real engaged couple.

Neither Sarah nor Raffe mentioned anything about the sabotage. Somehow they both knew that the fewer people they told the better.

They slipped into an easy conversation about a dozen topics. The beach, baseball teams, stories of Sarah when she was young. It all came very naturally. A few times Sarah even took Raffe's hand and squeezed it, and he rubbed her shoulder. Her parents took notice, smiling as Sarah and Raffe did these things, approving of the happy fake relationship.

"So, Raffe, tell us about yourself. We don't know much about you at all because our daughter has kept you a big secret," Michelle joked.

"Oh, well, let's see. The condensed version is I grew up in Europe, at boarding schools really. That's how I met Sarah's boss, Jasper. We were in boarding school together. I studied business and eventually opened my first restaurant in the U.S. a few years ago, and now I have half a dozen. I plan to open one in New York soon and hope that this contest helps me gain recognition as a serious chef. The rest is very boring really."

"Is that what your family is in? The food industry?" Michelle asked.

Raffe shook his head. "Pharmaceuticals, but I wasn't interested in that."

"Wait a minute. Washburn. Is that what you said your

last name is? As in Washburn Industries?" Bruce perked up.

"Yep," Raffe replied quietly.

Raffe hated being associated with his father's money. At some point in his life it would be nice if he could be recognized for his own work instead of his father's. Yes, he had gotten seed money from his father, but he'd grown the business tenfold since then on his own knowledge and business acumen.

"They make my blood pressure pills," Bruce said.

"Well, you'll have to come eat at one of my own restaurants when we get back home. The soothing food will help lower it even more," Raffe joked.

Her parents laughed and looked impressed with his humble synopsis of his life. Sarah also smiled, but she had already known all of these details. Of course, he'd left out the part about his ex-wife sucking the life out of him and almost leaving him bankrupt and being forced to rebuild from scratch.

Michelle looked at her watch. "I hate to say this, but we should really be leaving. The show people said we had to be back in the lobby by six to catch the ride back to the airport. We get to stay there overnight, in a suite!" Sarah's mother grabbed her purse and gave her daughter a tight hug. She turned to Raffe, opening her arms, and Raffe hugged her. "Welcome to the family. Take care of my daughter," she whispered in his ear.

Raffe shook Sarah's father's hand and walked him out. They declined his offer to accompany them to the lobby, so he stood on the deck and watched them walk off, hand in hand, a strange warmth swirling in his chest.

"Well, that went okay, right? I mean, think they believed it?" he asked Sarah as he walked back into the bungalow.

"Yeah, I think they believed it. I feel kind of bad for lying to them. I haven't lied to them before. I guess it's a good thing that they were only here for that short time." Sarah seemed preoccupied, standing at the door and staring out toward the ocean. "I could use some fresh air. I think I'll go for a walk."

She stepped onto the sand and walked toward the ocean. Two people had put beach chairs out, and she stopped next to them. Squinting, he saw that it was Kim and Dave, the homeless couple. Someone must have said something funny, because he heard their laughter drift in along with the soft lapping of the ocean.

A pang of envy shot through him. Kim and Dave had nothing but appeared to be the happiest couple on the show. Raffe had been born into money and wasn't even half as happy. What was missing? Was it the fact that he still longed for his father's approval? Or was something else missing from his life?

He envied Sarah's relationship with her family. They didn't have money, but maybe their close, loving relationship was better.

Down on the beach, Sarah had left Kim and Dave and walked down the beach. She looked pensive. Was she thinking about this Tommy guy?

Raffe grabbed a beer from the fridge. Did it matter what Sarah was thinking about? Not really. This whole relationship was fake, and the sooner it was over the better. A smile tugged at the corner of his lips as he popped the cap off the beer. Jasper would have a field day if he even suspected the tiny bit of jealousy that Raffe felt.

Speaking of Jasper... Raffe pulled out his phone. His boyhood friend would get a kick out of hearing about Raffe meeting Sarah's folks.

"Well, I met the parents, so this is serious, just like you wanted," he joked as soon as Jasper answered.

"What? Why are her parents on the island?"

"The show flew them in. It was only for a few hours. They're nice people, very down to earth. Her mother didn't like the engagement ring, though."

Jasper laughed. "I told you that thing was too big. Maybe she sensed it only cost fifty bucks. But did they buy it? I mean, that you are engaged?"

"I'm pretty sure they did. Turns out your old assistant is a pretty good liar. I let her do all the explaining. If they were staying any longer, we might have been in trouble, but it's good for now."

"I can't wait to hear what other surprises they have in store for you guys. Maybe they will throw you a wedding as a surprise?"

"Well, if that happens, you'll be reading about the cooking show contestant who stabbed himself in the eye to avoid getting married." Raffe hoped the show had no more surprises in store for them, though judging by what had happened so far, the producers did seem to like to spring things on them.

"Ha! Okay then. Well, congrats on meeting the parents. Almost like a real engagement, right? How are things going in close quarters with Sarah?"

"Awkward. I sleep on the couch." No sense in giving Jasper ammunition to tease him with. "How about you and Marly."

"These wedding details aren't my thing," Jasper said. "I can't wait until Sarah comes back so Marly can talk to her instead of me. But you know, I wouldn't change it for the world. I never realized how much was missing from my life until I met Marly. When the right girl comes along, it changes everything."

"I'm happy for you, bud," Raffe said.

"Thanks. Hey, Edward's been busy tormenting the crew at EightyEight, so he's been out of my hair. Thanks for that."

Raffe laughed, picturing Edward bossing around the crew. He'd have to call Darren and try to keep him from blowing a gasket. "Glad I could help you out."

"I gotta run. Keep me posted."

Raffe ended the call and finished his beer, his eyes on the surf and Jasper's words ringing in his head. Jasper had never realized what was missing until he met the right girl.

Raffe rummaged in the refrigerator for supper. Where was Sarah? He kept glancing out toward the beach. It was getting dark and she still wasn't back. Kim and Dave were gone too. Maybe they'd met up for drinks or something. Raffe didn't want a drink, so he used the opportunity to get ready in the bathroom. That way he'd be done and the room would be free for Sarah when she returned. Then he pulled out the sleeper sofa and got ready for bed.

As he lay there listening to the surf, almost on the verge of sleep, a niggle of a thought crossed his mind. A thought about what he really wanted in life and how he could take the steps to achieve it.

8

Sarah walked briskly along the gravel road toward the bridge, her stomach tight with nerves as she glanced around, hyperaware of her surroundings and ready to bolt if necessary. She had her phone held tightly to her ear, Marly on the other end. Thankfully there was a full moon that lighted the way. There were no streetlights on this part of the island.

"So we have no idea who is sabotaging us. Can you even believe this?" Sarah stopped walking and looked around, wondering if maybe this wasn't such a smart idea. The cab driver's warning about avoiding the area near the bridge rang in her head.

"Do you think maybe it's part of the contest? Like some kind of test or extra hurdle you have to navigate?" Marly asked, sounding concerned.

"Maybe. They do seem to like to throw curve balls at us. But there's a lot of money at stake. Maybe someone wants to make sure *they* win it by messing with the other contestants. We don't know if others have been sabotaged. I'm just glad that Raffe and I made it through the first two rounds. That, and the fact that we were able to pull off being engaged to my parents."

Marly laughed. "Well, maybe there's hope for you two yet! I mean, the bed with rose petals could have been a sign."

"Ha! Doubt it." Sarah scoffed at the idea. It had been easier than she thought to pretend to be engaged, but that had only been for a few hours. She and Raffe were two very different people, and after what happened with Harley, she had no interest in getting involved.

She should have known Harley, with his smooth talk and designer suits, would be nothing but trouble. But he had really hit it off with her family, especially her brother Tommy. Tommy and Harley had even hung out more than Harley and Sarah had.

Her heart ached at the thought of her younger brother and what Harley had done to him. Worse than anything was the knowledge that she had brought Harley into the family. Everything that had happened to Tommy was *her* fault, and this was her one chance to make it right.

She had fallen for Harley too hard and too fast, missing the warning signs, oblivious to the fact of what he really was. Too many stars in her eyes to ask where all his money came from. And when she finally learned Harley's money was the result of dealing drugs, it was too late for Tommy. Her brother, who had had a promising career in finance, was a full-blown heroin addict.

The last few years had been hell, with Tommy missing in action most of the time. He'd call every now and then, usually incoherent conversations that left Sarah feeling hollow and with massive anxiety. Sarah was thankful he never called their parents. She didn't want her mother to experience those conversations, though the hopeful look in her mother's eyes when she'd mentioned Tommy earlier had twisted a knife in her heart.

The last time she'd heard from Tommy had been almost a year ago. He had babbled on about going someplace warm. New York City winters could be brutal, especially if you had no home. He'd mentioned a restaurant that she'd traced to this very island.

That was one reason this contest was so appealing. The other was the prize money. That money could get Tommy into a good rehabilitation facility. If Tommy was still alive. But if he was, could Tommy be on this island? The tip from the cab driver and from Kim and Dave told her where to look.

If she couldn't find him on her own, maybe she'd show Kim a photo to learn if she knew Tommy. But for now she felt it was better to keep her extracurricular activities to herself. For all she knew, Kim and Dave were the saboteurs and would use the information about her quest to find Tommy to hurt her chances in the contest.

She'd be disqualified if the producers discovered that she'd left the confines of the resort.

"I gotta run. Cake tasting. Talk later!" Marly disconnected, and Sarah walked further along the roadway, closer to the bridge.

A dim light glowed from beneath the bridge, and she ventured off the road toward it, carefully sidestepping the driftwood and shells strewn along the beach.

The light was a fire in an old aluminum trash barrel. People stood around it. Odd, because it was still almost eighty degrees. As she drew closer, she saw bags strewn around and a few ripped tents. She'd found Tent City.

Her heart thudded as she cautiously approached. The people seemed harmless, just standing around talking. Soon someone noticed her, and a hush fell over the group. They eyed her warily as she approached.

"Hi. I'm looking for someone. Have any of you seen this guy?" She held out a photo of Tommy. It was a few years old, but she hoped he hadn't changed much. They all shook their heads no. But the looks in their eyes told her they might not tell her if they had seen him. These were people who didn't trust easily.

"Okay, thanks." She turned around, shoulders slumped. It had been too much to hope that she would run into her brother. Maybe he didn't even want her to find him. It wasn't as if he didn't know her number. If he wanted to get in touch, all he had to do was call.

As she walked back along the beach, memories of happier days surfaced. She and Tommy had been close.

And he'd had a bright promising career before the drugs. Oh well, no use thinking about the past. It was the future she could control, not the past.

But why hadn't he called in almost a year? She knew he was embarrassed about his situation, and she suspected that might have been one of the reasons he left New York. He'd always refused her help, except that one time he let her give him money. Maybe that was what he'd used for plane fare to fly down here. That still didn't explain why he hadn't called. Unless he couldn't for some reason.

Not wanting to think about reasons that would prevent Tommy from calling, Sarah squared her shoulders and hurried along, eager to get away from the seedy part of town as quickly as possible.

She checked the time on her phone. It was almost eleven. She really needed to get back to the resort before she got caught. She asked a few more people further down the beach huddled around a fire if they'd seen Tommy and then hurried away. No one had seen him.

Walking back to the resort seemed to take forever, but it gave Sarah time to clear her head. Everything with the contest was happening so fast. The fake engagement. Her parents. Looking for Tommy. It was too much.

She hurried to the bungalow, relieved to see that the lights were off. She made sure to enter as quietly as she could. She didn't want Raffe interrogating her about where she'd been. A snore from the area of the couch told her she hadn't woken him. Good, she'd just sneak into her room.

On the way she couldn't resist peeking over the top of the couch. Raffe snuggled under the sheet, his long eyelashes casting a shadow on his cheek. He looked like a little boy. Sweet and innocent. Hardly the hardened businessman and notorious playboy he was reputed to be.

For a second she wanted to wake him and tell him about Tommy. To get his take on it. Raffe was good at research and thinking things through. Maybe he'd have some ideas. But no, this was her problem, and she didn't want anyone to know about it. She took one last glance at Raffe before heading to the bedroom.

9

Raffe pushed the button on the coffee maker. He needed caffeine. Even though he had slept through the night, he was still a bit tired. He wasn't used to wearing pajamas and got all twisted up in them in the middle of the night. That didn't make for the most restful sleep. This whole sleeping on the sofa thing was annoying. He wished they could just ask for a two-bedroom bungalow, but that would be a dead giveaway that they weren't a couple.

Just as the coffee was ready Sarah came out of the bedroom. The morning light highlighted her flawless skin and golden hair, illuminating the subtle white-blond streaks that framed her face. Her amber eyes took on a golden hue in the morning light.

Maybe Raffe had never looked at her this closely, or maybe they'd been brought out by the hot tropical sun, but he noticed that she had a light sprinkling of freckles across the bridge of her nose and her cheeks, making her appear younger than her twenty-nine years.

The girls he dated always wore so much makeup he never even saw their actual skin. Lauren had even worn makeup to bed. Talk about wearing a mask. Sarah was always bare faced and so low maintenance.

"Coffee?" he asked her, reaching for the mugs.

"Sure. Thanks. What a beautiful day." She took the hot mug from him and walked toward the sliding glass door, looking out at the calm sea.

Raffe liked that she was always so positive and happy. Definitely qualities he wanted in a woman. Not that he was looking.

"So, did you have a good time with Dave and Kim last night? Did you do anything else? I fell asleep about an hour after you left." He sat down on the sofa bed, taking a long sip of coffee.

"Oh, no. I just stayed out on the beach and talked to them for a while and came back. I'm glad I didn't wake you when I came in."

Raffe wondered why she'd lie. He knew she'd gone somewhere else, because he'd watched her walk down the beach away from Kim and Dave. She'd also done a good job of lying to her parents. Maybe Sarah wasn't as sweet and innocent as she looked. But before he could ask where she'd been, a knock sounded on the door.

Sarah glanced at Raffe. He shrugged, and Sarah opened the front door. Jim, an assistant from the show, stood on the deck with his clipboard and headset on. He looked anxious and embarrassed. "Hi, guys. Sorry to bother you both so early, but there's an issue."

Raffe glanced at Sarah. The worry on her face was evident. What now?

"Issue? What kind of issue?" Had they figured out that he and Sarah weren't really engaged?

"You see, well, there's been a complaint about you. Someone claims they saw a person go into your side of the walk-in cooler during the last contest, and that is why you did so well. That you somehow got a look at the cards to tell you what to cook for each other."

"What?" Raffe and Sarah both shouted simultaneously.

"We didn't even win!" Sarah cried out.

"I know. But you did come in second. And Brenda—I mean, this person—well, it's just easier if you come with me."

Raffe and Sarah exchanged glances. So, Brenda had been the one who had complained. Raffe could tell by Sarah's eyes what she thought, which was most likely something like "I told you so!"

They dressed in lightning speed and followed Jim to Scott at the producer's office to defend themselves. Was Brenda behind the sabotage too? No, that didn't make sense. If Brenda had sabotaged them, she wouldn't want to call attention to herself like this. So had someone else conducted the sabotage? Maybe more than one couple was trying to rig the contest.

"What's this all about?" Raffe demanded as soon as

they entered the room. "We absolutely have not cheated."
Other than faking our engagement.

"I saw someone go into that cooler! You *are* cheating!"
Brenda yelled, pointing a red fingernail at Raffe and
Sarah.

"Calm down, calm down. I'm sorry that this has
happened. I don't want to accuse anyone, but of course I
do need to ensure that this is investigated," Scott
explained as he motioned for Brenda to take a seat.

"You believe her?" Sarah asked, her face red with frustration. "How are you going to investigate? Aside from
our word, what can you use for evidence to prove that
we aren't lying?"

"Did anyone look at the security tapes?" Jim asked,
pointing to the corner of the room where there was a
large monitor. The screen displayed the kitchen stadium,
now empty except for a few staff members checking that
the kitchens were properly stocked.

"Excellent idea. Let's take a look," Scott said, sitting
down at the monitor and typing something on the
keyboard.

They all gathered around the monitor to watch,
Brenda pushing her way in so she stood next to Scott and
directly in front of the monitor.

"Try camera six. That's the one in the back hall. We
installed it last minute; not even all the crew is aware of
it," Jim suggested to Scott.

They watched in silence. The tape showed several
people come and go, but they all went down the hallway.

No one entered the cooler. Then an overweight woman with platinum blond hair entered the frame. She pressed a large notebook to her breast and looked to be in a rush, darting into the walk-in cooler and coming back out shortly after, the notebook still clutched to her chest. Scott stopped the video and zoomed in on her face.

Raffe squinted as the face came into focus. The woman looked vaguely familiar. Beside him Sarah gasped. Then he realized who it was.

"Veronica?" he asked incredulously at the same time as Sarah.

What in the hell would Veronica St. James be doing there? And what in the world had happened to her? She had been Jasper's assistant up until several months ago, but back then she'd been much thinner. Raffe had never liked her. He'd been glad when Jasper fired her. But what was she doing here?

"Veronica, come to my office immediately," Scott barked into a two-way radio, a scowl on his face.

"She works here?" Sarah asked, her gaze darting from Scott to Raffe.

Scott nodded, and two seconds later Veronica entered the room, wearing the same sour look that she always had. The extra weight did not make it any more appealing.

"Were you in the walk-in area during yesterday's competition?" Scott asked her as she sat down.

"Yes, of course I was. You want me to do my job, right? I was in there to ensure that the domed items were lined up correctly so that no time was lost when the reveal came. Is something wrong?"

Just as she finished speaking, a loud squeaking mechanical sound echoed in the room, and an older woman in a wheelchair appeared in the doorway.

"What's this all about? We have a show to run!" she said in an irritated tone, glaring at Scott.

"Gertie," Scott's eyes were wide, as if he were terrified of the old woman. Was she someone important? Raffe had no idea but couldn't help but feel amused at Scott's reaction. Brenda, on the other hand, was not afraid.

"Look, lady, these two"—she stabbed her finger at Sarah and Raffe—"cheated with this Veronica person, and this tape proves it."

Gertie squinted at the tape. "I don't have time for this nonsense. Weren't these the two who had the foolish Peeps dessert? What do you think Veronica did, sneak in there and make that beautiful dessert display for them? Ha! Veronica was sent in there on my orders. She is to keep things moving along and make sure things are where they are supposed to be. She doesn't have time to make desserts or switch cards or whatever it is you think she did to help them cheat."

"But they all know each other!" Brenda screeched, causing Gertie to give her a sneer. "These two know Veronica!"

"They do all seem to know one another. I need to ensure for legal reasons everything is above board, right?" Scott asked Gertie, sounding unsure of himself and almost childlike.

"We know each other only from a previous work situation," Raffe said, giving Veronica a look of disdain.

"We are *not* friends with her," Sarah added. "Quite the opposite. We haven't seen or spoken to her in months."

"Scott, this nonsense has gone on long enough. So they all worked together before. Who cares? Let them have a reunion later on. Get the show started for today. I don't like my time being wasted, and I don't like Veronica being accused of trying to help these people cheat." With that, Gertie wheeled herself out of the room, leaving everyone else standing speechless.

They could all hear her say, "Peeps!" loudly, followed by a laugh, as she wheeled down the hall.

"Well, I guess that's that. Gertie makes the rules. However, Raffe and Sarah, I do not want to see you fraternizing with Veronica. If I do, you're off the show. And, Veronica, same goes for you. Everyone understand?" Scott gave them a hard look.

"But... but..." Brenda sputtered.

"And you," he glared at Brenda, "don't make accusations that you can't substantiate."

Raffe grabbed Sarah's hand and hustled her from the room, feeling the weight of Brenda's glare as they hurried down the hall.

VERONICA HUSTLED to catch up to Gertie as she wheeled herself into her office. For an older woman she sure was fast in that thing!

"Thanks for sticking up for me back there. Usually I'm on my own," she said as she watched Gertie maneuver herself behind her desk.

"I'm not sure why I stuck up for you. I know how you feel. You wouldn't behave this way if things had been different for you as a child. Remember, I had a rough childhood too. And I did some pretty crappy things to people on my way up. So, I don't know, I'm old and I guess maybe I feel like I need to atone for my sins now by trying to save you from continuing down the wrong path. Sort of a reverse karma kind of thing." She shivered and pulled her shawl closer around her shoulders, scowling up at the air conditioning vent.

"Well, I appreciate—"

Gertie's hand shot up, cutting her off. "You have a lot of potential. If you used your anger in a positive way, I'm sure your life would improve and become what you've always dreamed it would be. You had dreams when you were younger, right? Just like I did. And our parents, teachers, friends… they all crapped all over our dreams. No one helped us. So do what I did." Gertie leaned forward. "Help yourself. I believe in you."

Veronica mumbled, "Thank you," under her breath and backed out of the room. How did this old bat know she'd had dreams when she was younger? In fact, that was all she had had—just dreams. And stupid ones at that, at least according to anyone she told. After a while she'd stopped dreaming all together. But what if…?

Nah, it was stupid. Things wouldn't improve for her. Gertie was crazy.

And she knew better than to listen to anyone. She'd always had only herself to depend on. Like when she'd left home as soon as she had turned eighteen. It was one of the best moves she'd ever made, even if she had been totally unprepared to support herself.

The weight had come flying off between all the walking she did around the city and her lack of eating three meals a day. She had been lucky if she could afford one meal a day. She'd picked up a waitressing job, gone to night school. In no time at all she'd transformed herself into a skinny size two and landed a job as assistant to the chief executive officer of Draconia Fashions. Of course, then she'd been fired, but that hadn't been her fault.

The fact that she had gained almost all of her weight back after being fired should have humbled her, but instead it had made her even more bitter than ever.

Hmmm… come to think of it, her problems had begun when she'd started trying to make Jasper see how wrong Marly was for him. Okay, she had played some underhanded tricks back then, but she was trying to save Jasper. Except Jasper and Marly seemed really happy now. And her life had grown steadily more miserable.

Maybe Gertie *was* right. Maybe she should stop

putting all her energy into trying to ruin people's lives and focus on improving her own.

Pffft. Veronica laughed. What fun would she have if she were nice? Besides, no one was ever nice to *her*. She was fine being all alone. Just like always.

10

"I cannot believe *she* is there!"

Sarah held the phone away from her ear so that Marly's screech wouldn't burst her ear drums. She'd called Marly first thing after exiting Scott's office. Veronica had almost screwed things up for Marly, and now Sarah was positive she had been sabotaging her and Raffe. "It's crazy, right? And, get this, she is big now. As in she must be eating ten bags of M&Ms a day. No more sky-high stilettos either. Flats. She's so different!"

"Okay, never mind the picture of the rose petals on the bed, I need a picture of Veronica! After all the times she called me fat, maybe this is karma in action!" Marly said.

Sarah agreed with her. Karma had definitely paid Veronica a visit. She had always been nasty to everyone when they had worked together—well, everyone except for Jasper. But she'd been especially nasty to Marly.

Ending her call with Marly, Sarah walked into the bungalow, still shaking her head as she looked at Raffe.

"I can't believe Veronica works for the show. And she has access to all the behind-the-scenes stuff. *And* she was seen in the cooler, so obviously she switched the desserts." Sarah snapped her fingers. "Of course! I should have known when I saw the M&Ms. Veronica has a penchant for them."

Sarah paced the length of the bungalow while Raffe sat on the sofa, turning this way and that to follow her progress, a glass of orange juice on the table in front of him.

"I agree it appears more than random. Do you think she got this job knowing we'd be contestants? That seems impossible. What experience does she have, and how would she even know we were contestants?"

"Who knows?" Sarah flapped her arms. Raffe's cool demeanor bugged her. Didn't he get ruffled about anything? "She skulks around. She knew lots of stuff about Marly because she's sneaky."

"True. But we can't confront her about it without taking the risk of being tossed off the show. It seems like that Gertie woman calls the shots, and she definitely was protective of Veronica." Raffe settled back into the chair, his face grim. "She might even suspect that we aren't really engaged."

Sarah nodded her head slowly. Raffe was right. If they approached Veronica about it, she'd probably make up some story or do something sneaky that would get them kicked off. "I don't think she knows, because if she did, she'd probably tell them and try to get us booted. But I agree, we don't want anyone looking too closely at us. Best to just keep an eye on her and make sure she can't mess with us anymore."

"It's possible it's not even her. I know, long shot. But Brenda told on us, so it would appear she has it in for us too," Raffe said.

"Trust me, Veronica being here is no coincidence. I don't know; this is so confusing. I guess we need to keep an eye on both of them!" Sarah pulled a glass from the cabinet and stabbed it under the water dispenser built into the refrigerator. This was so frustrating! Not only did she have to worry about winning the contest, now she had to keep on the lookout for Veronica.

"I agree. But, for right now we need to get to the kitchen for the next contest." Raffe finished his orange juice, and they both put their glasses in the sink and headed out to the conference center.

Sarah developed the usual case of nerves as they traveled the path to the entrance to the kitchens. Today there would be a live audience consisting mostly of other guests from the resort and a few locals. As they entered the kitchen, Sarah glanced at the audience. Men in Hawaiian shirts, women in colorful sundresses. Everyone looked casual and relaxed.

She nodded to the other contestants and took her place at the cooking station while waiting for Landon to tell them about today's contest.

"Attention! Today's challenge is bacon. No, not baking, *bacon*. You will prepare your bacon three different ways for the judges, incorporating it into three separate appetizers. Use your creativity, because the team with the least impressive dish will be going home. The challenge starts… *now*!"

"Yes!" Raffe was already unwrapping the thick slabs of bacon that had been set out for them. "If there's one food I love, it's bacon. Doesn't everyone love bacon?" He glanced at Sarah.

"Yeah, you love it, but any ideas on appetizers," Sarah asked him as she started to cut the bacon into slices. "Actually, should I be slicing them this thick?" She had a few ideas about the bacon but wanted to hear what Raffe had to say. He owned so many upscale restaurants that they most likely had more than one trendy bacon appetizer. Plus, she wanted to see if he could take the lead or if it would be all up to her for the entire contest. Not that she minded. She was used to going it on her own with no one else to depend on.

"Bacon cheese balls. Bacon-wrapped sliders. And maple-candied bacon. How does that sound? And yes, keep slicing them exactly like you are. That's great!"

Apparently bacon was Raffe's thing. He was in his element, explaining that he'd worked with his chefs on bacon appetizer recipes because they were a key part of his menu in all the trendy locations like Los Angeles, Miami, and Boston.

"All these recipes are the most popular on my menus, so I think we're a shoo-in," he explained.

They worked seamlessly side by side, Sarah following his instructions to the letter as well as making a few suggestions that he immediately incorporated, causing her face to flush with pride when he commented on how they improved the dish and asked if he could employ them in his restaurants.

By the time Landon bellowed that time was up, Sarah was just finishing the last of the garnish. She stood back, chancing a look at the other contestants' plates. Their dishes weren't as expertly plated, nor did they seem to have as much variety. Hope swelled in her chest. They had this, maybe would even win.

As usual, Landon took forever, chatting about bacon, making a comment about each appetizer and then drawing out the announcement. Unlike the cooking portion that was filmed in one swoop, the announcements and tasting took longer as the judges asked for retakes when they flubbed their lines.

After what seemed an eternity, Landon finally grabbed the microphone, smoothed his hair, and nodded to the cameras to start rolling.

"Contestants, are you ready?"

The chefs all nodded and shuffled around nervously in front of their dishes.

Landon turned to the audience. "Audience, are you ready?"

"Yes!" The audience waved and bounced in their chairs.

Landon turned back to the camera, smiling. "Well then, without further ado… the winner is…"

Sarah's heart pounded on her ribcage as he inserted the usual dramatic pause.

"Team One—Raffe and Sarah!"

Sarah's hands flew to her cheeks. They'd won their first challenge! She turned to Raffe. He was happy, smiling. Sarah felt like jumping up and down, oh wait, she *was* jumping up and down.

"Congratulations, you two!" Landon came to them, a cameraman trailing behind him. "Now, let's see a nice big victory kiss!"

Sarah stopped midjump. Did he say kiss? Her eyes jerked from Landon's dorky smiling face to Raffe's panic-stricken one.

Don't panic. Keep smiling. Breathe. Think of a way to get out of it.

Landon raised his brow at them expectantly, the audience leaning forward in their seats. Everyone waited for them to kiss. There was no way to get out of it without giving away the fact that they weren't a couple.

She stepped closer to Raffe, her pulse thudding. Okay, a quick peck should satisfy them.

She stood on the tips of her toes, tilting her head up as Raffe bent his down.

Warm breath ghosted across her face, and then his lips were on hers. Warm, soft and… delicious. His arm snaked around her waist, and she vaguely heard the audience utter a collective, "Awww," as she stepped in closer.

THE KISS WASN'T anything like Raffe had anticipated. He'd expected Sarah's lips to be stiff and cold. But they were soft and... pliable. He only meant to give her a quick peck, but he found himself pulling her in close, deepening the kiss by instinct.

Apparently he'd let his lips linger longer than they should have, because the next thing he knew, Landon cleared his throat and cracked a joke about waiting for the honeymoon that elicited a burst of laughter from the audience and crew.

He pulled back, heart racing and warmth flooding his veins. Sarah's face was flushed, her eyes half closed and dreamy. The kiss had definitely affected him. Had it affected her too?

Suddenly embarrassed and confused, he jerked away from her and started busy work, wiping their knives and scrubbing down the countertops.

"That was luck, I think. The bacon, I mean. I have so many variations on my menus it was easy to come up with the dishes." Raffe tried to talk his way through the awkwardness.

"Right. Those are delicious. I can see why they are favored in your restaurants."

"Yeah, the maple-candied one is a personal favorite. It looks like Durkin really likes it too."

Raffe nodded toward the food critic, who sat with a pile of the candied bacon in front of him. He bit into a piece of it, eyes closed and head leaning slightly back. Sarah and Raffe burst into laughter.

"It's definitely something I'm going to try a recipe variation of when I get home," Sarah said. "I mean, if you don't mind."

"Sure, have at it." Raffe wondered if Sarah would go back to work for Jasper when they got back or seek out that chef position she hoped for. There was no doubt she was an excellent cook, and it seemed she could handle a kitchen. In fact, she'd be a great addition to his new restaurant.

They finished cleaning up and headed to the bungalow. Raffe slowed and let Sarah go in ahead of him so he could make a quick call to Jasper outside alone.

"I'll be there in a sec," Raffe said as he pulled out his phone and pressed the contact for Jasper.

"You again? I feel like we're back in school, you know, when you'd call me nonstop even though I was in the next room over from you?" Jasper joked. "Is the contest that boring?"

Raffe, remembering those days, laughed. When he was in New York they saw each other almost daily. Now that he thought about it, they didn't speak on the phone much between seeing each other so often and texting.

"I just had a quick question for you about Sarah. Is she coming back to work for you after this?"

"Well, I think so. I mean, I left it open to her. She's the best assistant I've ever had, but she's totally overqualified for the role. Especially with the cooking. I think she should pursue a job in that line. Why do you ask?"

Raffe hesitated with his answer. He knew his friend could read him, and his answer might encourage Jasper's scheme to fix him up. He didn't need that, because then Jasper would tell Marly, and things might get blown out of proportion.

"Just wondering. Something was mentioned in the contest about jobs. I just wasn't sure. I figured she was going back to work for you. Thanks for the info."

He felt bad lying, but he knew in this situation it was best. Same for telling Jasper about the kiss. It was best not to mention it. He ended the call as he walked into the bungalow.

11

Sarah grabbed two ice-cold bottles of beer from the fridge in their bungalow, handed one to Raffe, and then plopped down on the opposite end of the sofa.

"We made it again," she said, leaning over to tap her bottle against Raffe's in celebration. The unexpected kiss at the end, still fresh in her mind, had created a new level of awkwardness, especially now that they were alone in the bungalow.

"Yes, only four more to go. We might actually win this thing," Raffe said.

Pride bloomed in Sarah's chest. It turned out they actually were a good team, despite the reservations she'd had when she'd agreed to enter the contest. Now they'd survived the elimination and two challenges. They actually had a real shot at winning.

"We should try to anticipate what the next challenge will be, you know, try to prepare for it." Sarah was trying to keep her mind on the contest, but her thoughts kept drifting to the kiss. "Your research has really helped us with food pairings, so we should try to leverage that."

"Thanks. I think the fact that you think quick on your feet helps too. Gets us up and running fast," Raffe said. "I think as long as we just stay calm and communicate we can win."

Sarah sipped her beer, looking at Raffe out of the corner of her eye. Should she mention the kiss? She wanted to forget about the darn thing, but all she could do was think about it. Obviously the kiss wasn't a big deal to Raffe. He acted completely normal. Still, shouldn't she say something to clear the air?

"I think I'll take a shower now," was all that came out of her mouth instead.

Sarah shut the bathroom door and leaned up against it. This was all becoming too stressful. First the show makes them shack up together, and then they make them kiss. What was next?! She called Marly, hoping that she didn't have an anxiety attack in the process.

"They made us kiss, and I don't know what to do. This is so awkward." She blurted as soon as Marly answered.

"Um, what? You kissed? *Oh my God!* How was it? What was it like? Like a movie kiss or a peck on the cheek? *I need the details!*" Marly's voice rose with excitement.

"God no! Not like a movie kiss. But not a peck either. Okay, maybe kind of like a movie kiss, but not a really long one. Well, kind of long, I guess. It was like one that Big and Carrie would have after they hadn't seen each other in a while when they weren't hooking up and were in other relationships but then they see each other and want to hook up." Sarah knew Marly would know exactly what she meant. They had both binge watched the *Sex and the City* series together.

"Umm, whoa! Okay, well, I guess there isn't much you can do about it, right? Just go with it. That's so awkward!" Marly laughed.

"I can't believe you talked me into this contest. I'm coming home!"

"No you're not! You're there to win. So you had to kiss? Big deal. Just act like nothing happened. Let me guess, that's how Raffe acted, like nothing happened?"

"Yes. Which makes it even more awkward," Sarah lowered her voice, hoping Raffe wasn't standing outside the bathroom door with his ear up to it.

"Look, it's not as big a deal as you think. I mean, they all assume you guys are engaged. Just pretend you're acting. It's all an act. I mean, it's kind of true anyway, you're acting engaged. Maybe that will help you get through the horrible ordeal of kissing Raffe Washburn."

Sarah rolled her eyes. Horrible ordeal? She wished. She wished she could just forget about it and act normal. But she'd *felt* something. Probably one-sided, though. Raffe was hot. He had his pick of women. And he acted as though nothing had happened. Marly was right. That's what she needed to do too. Act as if the kiss meant nothing.

She disconnected and turned the shower on, hoping it would wash her anxiety away.

VERONICA SLAMMED her foot down on the ant running along the sidewalk, wishing it was Sarah. Damn it! Sarah and Raffe had won yet another contest and would move onto the next round. All her attempts to sabotage them had backfired so far, and to make matters worse, Tanner wouldn't stop texting and calling.

Ugh... and that kiss. Veronica rolled her eyes even though no one was around to see. How sappy sweet. If Veronica had had doubts that Raffe and Sarah were a real couple, they'd been put to rest with that stupid kiss. No one had ever kissed Veronica like that.

She pulled a handful of M&Ms, warm from the heat of the day, from her pocket. She opened her mouth and popped the whole handful in then noticed the red, green, and blue spots on her palm from the coating. "Melts in your mouth not in your hand, my ass!"

Rounding the corner, she spotted Brenda and Dick. Their conversation stopped abruptly, and they each stepped back to let her pass. Veronica continued on until the path wound out of sight, then darted behind a tall silver bismarck palm so she could hear the conversation. She scratched her arm on the rough razor-like leaves jutting from the trunk. The sharp scent of the mulch wafted up, and she looked down. Damn, she'd gotten mulch stains on her white ballet flats. A tiny gecko poised on the leaf in front of her. "What are you looking at?" she snarled, and it scurried away, giving her the satisfaction of having scared it off. Veronica leaned forward to listen in on the conversation.

"Yes, Dick, I'm positive they're cheating, and I know that Veronica woman is helping them. Didn't you think that was obvious when we were in Scott's office?"

"I dunno. I mean, I guess it was an odd coincidence that they know each other." Dick didn't sound convinced, or interested, in Brenda's accusation.

"Coincidence my ass! And you know what else? I think I saw Sarah leave the resort the other night. Late. And you know that's against the rules! I almost told Scott, but I don't want to tell him anything again unless I have proof!"

"What do you mean you saw her leaving the resort? Where would she go?" Dick asked.

"How do I know?" Brenda snapped. "Maybe she has a mole who lives here on the island and works at the resort that she had to meet. Maybe she's selling stories about the inner workings of the contest to The Enquirer. Whatever. It doesn't sound like a coincidence *now*, does it!"

"Brenda, I really don't care one way or the other. Let's go." Dick sounded exhausted.

Veronica didn't doubt that being married to Brenda

was tiresome. She was a busybody who always bugged others with her gossiping. She had even been told more than once to stop talking so much during the contests. But this gossip had given her some good intelligence on Sarah. Was Sarah sneaking out? If so, why? And where was she going?

Veronica peeked between the palm fronds to make sure no one was around before slipping out from behind the tree and heading to her room. Her plans had just changed, but she needed a nap. She wouldn't get much sleep tonight, because she'd be following Sarah's every move to find out exactly what was going on. As she hurried along, she almost plowed over a slow idiot pedestrian in her way.

"Whoa, slow down!" a deep voice said. "What's the emergency? You run out of clean pans?"

Veronica eyed the smart-ass dishwasher up and down. For some reason he reminded her of Jasper Kenney, her old boss. He had the same blue eyes and chiseled jaw and was tall like Jasper. But that's where the resemblance ended. He clearly didn't have the billions of dollars Jasper did. He also looked like he hadn't eaten in a month. *And*, he was a dishwasher, not a CEO.

"Have you ever thought of hosting the nightly comedy show here instead of scrubbing pans?" she asked, her face cracking into a sarcastic smile as she stared at him intently, waiting for him to break and look away in fear like everyone else did.

"Yes, actually I have. But I heard it was draining."

Veronica's eyes narrowed. What the heck? He didn't back down, nor did he break eye contact. She should be insulted. So why did she think his comment was kind of funny? She snorted, the closest thing she'd let herself come to a laugh.

Wait, this guy was her underling. Shouldn't she reprimand him for insubordination or something? Now, what was his name?

"You should put something on that. It could get infected." The dishwasher pointed to her arm, and Veronica looked down at the bloody scratch from the palm tree. No one had ever expressed concern for her before. Was this some kind of trick?

She looked up, ready to confront him and demand to know what he was up to, but he was already halfway down the path, the sun falling on his broad shoulders as he whistled a cheerful tune.

Veronica stared after him. Oh well, she'd yell at him later. No one had a right to be that cheerful.

TJ SHUFFLED DOWN THE PATH, whistling softly under his breath. That Veronica sure was a piece of work. The entire kitchen staff was terrified of her. They referred to her as "the tyrant" but, of course, never when she was around.

She was always yelling and complaining about something. As if someone like her should have anything to complain about. But she found plenty. Either they weren't getting clean pots out to the kitchens fast enough, or the utensils weren't clean enough, or the kitchen was too hot or too cold. She was never satisfied.

Veronica acted as though everything was such a big deal, but TJ guessed someone like her had no concept of real hardship. Not like he did. But still, he sensed something just beneath the surface. Like maybe there was a reason she acted so bitchy, and maybe there was a nicer Veronica just under the surface, struggling to emerge.

He had to admit her quick-witted insults always made him chuckle, which usually infuriated her, and *that* made him chuckle even more.

But *her* struggles were not his concern. He had his own issues.

"Hi, handsome. What's new?" TJ grinned as he turned to see the familiar face of Gertie O'Rourke beaming up at him from her wheelchair. Gertie was one of the few people associated with the show that deigned to speak with him. One of the few who even knew his name. Normally, he preferred to keep his head down and his mouth shut, but somehow he'd found himself drawn to the feisty old lady.

"Hey, beautiful, how's your day been so far? Any new gossip?" he asked her as he stooped to be closer to her eye level.

"Meh, no good gossip really. Today's contest was about bacon. Bacon! What kind of contest is that for a real chef? These young ones don't know how to put the pressure on, that's for sure!"

TJ laughed. He loved this woman's fire. She might have a disability, but she was in no way weak. The disability had only made her stronger, he imagined.

"Well, don't you run the show? I mean, don't you decide what the contests are?"

"I'm supposed to, but this corporation has things all political. Got these young yahoo executive producers who think they know everything above me giving orders. I don't like it at all. In fact, I'm thinking of cutting out and doing my own thing, sweetie. What do ya think about that?"

TJ grinned at her as her face beamed.

"I think that's exactly what you should do, Gertie. And if you do, you'd better take me with you!"

He kissed her hand and watched her as she wheeled away, giggling, his heart bursting with happiness that he'd made her smile.

12

Raffe sat on the bungalow's deck steps, his feet dug into the hot sand, and tried not to think about Sarah in the shower. For some reason the thought terrified him. That's why he'd left. How stupid was that? It wasn't as if he'd never showered with a woman before.

But this was different. He was depending on Sarah to win the contest. He needed her. And, well, he liked her too. But that stupid kiss had changed everything. No wonder Sarah was acting strange. She had that boyfriend, Tommy, her mother had mentioned. Maybe he wasn't really an ex, maybe her mother just assumed that because she was supposed to be engaged to Raffe now. Poor kid was probably riddled with guilt over kissing him.

The sun cast long shadows behind the bungalow as he walked to the shoreline, the sand turning cold and wet as he got closer to the pounding surf. The humidity increased, and Raffe tasted the salt on his tongue as he looked out over the aqua-blue sea, watching the white dot of a cruise ship glide along the horizon.

He stood for several minutes as the color of the sky transitioned from blue to purple while the sun dipped further behind him. The sunrises here on the beach were awesome, but sunsets could be just as pretty.

He started back toward the resort. He didn't want to go into the bungalow yet, so he veered onto the stone path that meandered along the edge of the resort. Shaded by palms and lined with tropical plantings, it was darker here, cooler.

As he came upon one of the alcoves situated along the path, he heard someone crying and noticed a hunched figure sitting alone on the stone bench. He recognized Gina as he drew closer.

"Gina? Are you okay?" he asked, unsure of what to do. Damn! He hated when women cried. It always made him feel useless. Plus it usually meant drama, and if there was anything Raffe hated, it was drama. But it was too late to turn around now. He'd already opened his big mouth, and Gina was looking up at him with luminous watery eyes.

"Hi, Raffe. Sorry, I didn't hear you." She dabbed at her wet eyes with a tissue, black mascara marks running down her cheeks.

"What's going on? Are you all right?" Raffe sat down beside her.

"It's just, oh, I don't know, Raffe. Here we are in this beautifully romantic resort, in these gorgeous bungalows, and all Tony can think about is if the TV gets ESPN. He's just so uninterested in me! I may as well not even exist."

Raffe chuckled over the sports comment, and Gina started sobbing again. As usual, he'd done the wrong thing.

"Oh no, I'm sorry. I didn't mean to make you more upset. The ESPN comment made me laugh. Don't all guys like ESPN? I know I do, but I'm sure Tony is interested in you. I mean, you are married after all."

"How do you do it? How do you stay so happy and interested? You and Sarah. I watch you both. You get along so well. Always making one another laugh! And it is so obvious that you are physically attracted to each other, even after you've been together for a few years."

Was it obvious? Sarah was pretty, and he had to admit there was a bit of an attraction there. Okay, given how his body reacted to the kiss, a lot of an attraction. But they were just friends.

Raffe hadn't considered how he and Sarah appeared to others. They must be doing a good job faking it. Ironic though that a woman who was having marriage troubles was asking him how he and his fake fiancé remained so happy.

"Well, I guess it's just that we trust each other. And we don't take each other for granted. I mean, we're lucky that we found each other. And she's funny. She makes me laugh all the time. She is very down to earth." Raffe stopped abruptly. Was he gushing? The words had just tumbled out. True words.

"Well, he doesn't even seem interested if I flirt with other men," Gina blew her nose into the tissue.

So *that's* why she'd been flirting with him—to make Tony jealous. Raffe felt a stab of pity at her desperation.

"You know, Gina, I guess maybe the key is to not try too hard. I mean, just be yourself. Don't be a flirt. That might actually push Tony away. Just be honest and tell him how you feel. Maybe he doesn't know you want to spend time doing other things instead of watching TV. You two have been together a lot longer than Sarah and I have, and sometimes relationships just need a boost. If sports are such a big deal to him, maybe you should suggest that you go to that romantic outdoor bar down by the water. There's a TV there, and you can have a nice night out and watch sports at the same time."

Gina's face lighted. "You really think so? That sounds like a good compromise." She dabbed at her cheeks, wiping off the muddy mascara tracks.

"Give it a try. Honesty is usually the best policy," Raffe said.

"Thank you so much! I never thought that maybe I was pushing Tony away instead of making him jealous. I love the idea of going to that bar! In fact, I'm going to go ask him now if he wants to go. Wish me luck!"

They both stood, and Gina threw her arms around him, thanking him again. Raffe was a bit taken by surprise but managed to hug back before she pushed away and ran off down the path.

Raffe's heart swelled watching her. He hoped his advice would mend their marriage. As he sat there, a strange feeling came over him. Maybe he needed to take some of his own advice. Was he really being honest with himself about how he felt about Sarah?

THE AIR in the back room of the kitchen was heavy with steam from the industrial automatic dishwasher. The rubber-mat-covered floor was soaked, and Veronica smelled the sweat of a hard day's work as she stood in front of the stainless steel table where one of the dishwashers loaded another tray to feed into the washer.

"What? No, I don't know his name. That's why I am asking *you*, you idiot. He works nights, and he looks like he would blow away in a strong wind he's so thin." Veronica had lost her patience with the incompetent kitchen staff over trying to learn the name of that snarky dishwasher she kept running into. No one seemed to know him. Didn't these people talk to each other?

She stormed out of the kitchen, pushing the steel swinging door so hard it slammed into the wall as she swore under her breath. She'd have to deal with that dishwasher later. She needed to check on Sarah again to make sure she hadn't left the bungalow.

As she turned onto the dimly lit path that led from

the resort's kitchen toward the bungalows, she saw two figures embracing in one of the romantic alcoves. Something about it looked suspicious. Slowing down, she stepped sideways behind a large palm tree, peeping her head out from behind it to watch.

Veronica couldn't believe her eyes. Raffe and Gina were hugging. Or kissing. Or at least doing something that they shouldn't be!

She pulled out her phone and aimed the camera, snapping off a few shots before ducking back behind the tree. Her spirits rose in triumph. She finally had something that she could use against them!

She didn't know how she could use the photos, but maybe fooling around with another contestant's spouse was against the rules. She made a mental note to look that up.

She turned and walked the long way around to the bungalows, casually strolling past Sarah and Raffe's, hoping to catch Sarah sneaking out. Nope. Veronica could see her through the sliding glass doors, sitting leisurely on the couch and flipping through a magazine. Probably one of those local tourist attraction publications the hotel left in every room. Maybe she wasn't going to sneak out tonight.

Her phone dinged in her hand, and she almost dropped it. She jerked her head up, hoping it hadn't alerted Sarah. No, she continued paging through the magazine. Veronica scurried out of view, looking at the display.

Damn, it was a text from Tanner.

Use the secret weapon. Or else.

13

The next day Sarah's morning coffee was disrupted by a sharp knock on the door. She was actually kind of glad for a distraction. Raffe had been acting weird, and the morning had been filled with awkward conversation punctuated by long silences.

The friendship she'd felt growing between them had been stunted, and she suspected it was all because of that stupid kiss. She wanted to tell him the kiss didn't matter, she wanted things to go back to the way they were. But somehow she couldn't get the words out. She was afraid that was because the words weren't true and that somewhere deep down inside the kiss *had* mattered.

So when Jim knocked on the door and summoned them to Scott's office, she was almost relieved.

On the way, Jim apologetically informed them that yet again there was an accusation against them about cheating, and Sarah guessed correctly as to who was behind it: Brenda.

"This is really starting to get ridiculous," Sarah said as they entered Scott's office, hoping no one noticed that her voice was trembling. She had an idea what this was about and hoped that she was wrong.

"You left the resort property the night before last, and you're not supposed to! It's against the rules! Cheater!" Brenda, who was already seated in the most comfortable guest chair, screeched as soon as they stepped into the office.

"Do you have proof that she left?" Scott asked Brenda, sounding a bit annoyed with the situation.

"Well, no. But I saw her!" Brenda replied, pointing her finger accusingly at Sarah.

Sarah's mind raced. Okay, think up an excuse. No wait, don't say anything. She can't prove it. Oh crap! We cannot lose the contest over this. Maybe it was better to keep her mouth shut. She was not a good liar.

"Sorry to burst your bubble, Brenda, but Sarah was with me. All night." Raffe put his arm around Sarah and winked. "Believe me, I would have noticed if she left."

Relief washed over her. Raffe had saved the day. Immediately following her relief, guilt started to kick in. Raffe knew she hadn't been there, but he was covering for her. Is this what it feels like when someone actually has your back? The only one who had ever looked out for her was Tommy. It felt good to have someone to depend on.

"Brenda, I've had enough of your antics, okay? Your accusations have cost us money and time, and so far nothing has come of them. If I were you, I'd focus on my cooking. You're barely squeaking by as it is. This is the last time I want to hear about any assumptions you have regarding who is doing what." With a wave of his hand, Scott dismissed her. He then turned to Raffe and Sarah. "I apologize for this, again. I have to follow up on all of these types of issues. I'm sure you understand. Better get a run on; the next contest starts in fifteen minutes."

Sarah and Raffe both thanked Scott and left, Sarah breathing a huge sigh of relief as she closed the office door behind her.

RAFFE DIDN'T KNOW why Brenda hated them so much. Maybe she was doing similar things to other contestants. Whatever. All he knew was that he couldn't let Sarah's nighttime wanderings get them kicked off, so he'd pretended she was with him in the bungalow.

But he had to wonder where Sarah had gone the other night. Maybe she had gone off the property to meet that ex-boyfriend Tommy. Or maybe she was just going for a stroll and wandered too far. Anyway, he couldn't ask her now. They needed to focus on cooking.

They went through the usual routine, sweating it out in front of the cameras while Landon enjoyed his on-air time and drew out the announcement of the challenge.

This time they were tasked with creating a tropical island dish.

Seafood immediately came to mind, and Raffe went through his mental index of recipes. Tilapia. Mahi Mahi. Grouper.

Sarah was already one step ahead of him, already grabbing a variety of seafood and bringing it back to their station. Shrimp, lobster, Mahi Mahi, and octopus. Octopus could be a challenge to cook right, but maybe Sarah knew what she was doing.

He started up the Jenn-Air grill while Sarah got busy whisking sauces. It was getting so they didn't even have to talk about who did what anymore.

Sarah was a whiz at creating marinades and dipping sauces, which was perfect because Raffe wasn't so good at that. Raffe, on the other hand, seemed to have some kind of sixth sense about when meat would be done, and his selections always came out perfect. Their engagement might be fake, but their skills really did complement each other. They made a pretty impressive team.

"What do you think we should do with the octopus? Grill it?" he asked her, leery of doing so. Octopus had a very small window for how long it could be cooked, and if cooked one second longer, it became tough as a tire. At the same time, grilling it would probably be different than any other team's approach.

"I think grilling is risky but worth it. You can do it; just go easy. Maybe sear it, and I'll make a dipping sauce."

Raffe nodded. Searing was a good idea. He only

hoped he didn't overdo it, because it could be their last challenge if he did.

He kept his eyes glued to the octopus, knowing that Sarah was watching him out of the corner of her eye. Instead of it irritating him, he was relieved. He knew if he did something wrong she'd tell him immediately. It was like a welcome system of checks and balances. It was critical they get this right, because if he ruined the food, they weren't allowed to start a new dish, no matter how much time was left on the clock.

He finished up the dishes, and Sarah plated them as he passed them along to her, adding sauces and various garnishes that added a punch of color. She drizzled the sauces in a funky design and finished by wiping the edges of the plates with a clean towel.

Yep, she'd make a fine head chef at one of his restaurants.

The staff took the tasting dishes to the judges, and Raffe's pulse notched up as they took their time sampling each dish, sometimes bending their heads together to discuss something. He paid special attention when it came to their dish, watching as they speared the octopus with their forks, scrutinized it from all angles, and finally tasted it.

Raffe wasn't sure but he thought that Durkin, by far the pickiest of the judges, made a face when he bit into the octopus. He recalled a review Durkin had written in his weekly food column for The New York Times about a restaurant's shrimp dish, claiming it had been one of the worst dishes he had ever had and that the shrimp tasted like burnt rubber dipped in raw sewage. The restaurant had been shuttered several weeks later.

"Ladies and gentlemen, our judges have the results!" Landon preened for the cameras. "Last time we announced the winners first. This time we'll start with the losers."

The audience oohed.

"But first, every team's dish was wonderful in many ways. It was a hard decision. And such variety…"

Raffe zoned out as Landon blabbed on about the various tastes and how they were judged on taste, inventiveness, and presentation.

"…and even in this close competition, someone must lose. In this case, the team with the lowest score missed the mark on presentation." Landon paused. "Team Six, Dick and Brenda… I'm sorry, but you're going home."

Brenda shrieked. "But—"

Dick grabbed her arm and Raffe heard him whisper, "Shush… we don't want to be sore losers."

Raffe glanced at Sarah and found her struggling not to smile. He shouldn't feel so triumphant, but it served Brenda right. Better yet, Raffe and Sarah wouldn't be going home!

Landon turned to the audience. "I always hate to see good chefs sent home. But there can be only one winner here. And we're closer than ever to the final challenge. So now, let's celebrate as I announce the winners of this challenge… Team One, Raffe and Sarah! They created a seared octopus with a jalapeño-based dipping sauce that the judges agreed was one of the best they've ever tasted. Even Franz Durkin."

Landon's last comment elicited laughter from the audience as Sarah launched herself excitedly into Raffe's arms. Caught up in the excitement, he spun her around a few times before putting her down. They were all smiles until they heard the chanting from the crowd.

"Kiss! Kiss! Kiss! Kiss!"

Raffe looked at Sarah. The panicked look on her face mirrored how he felt. Their smiles froze.

They must look like idiots just standing there. They needed to act like a real engaged couple. Maybe just a quick peck wouldn't hurt.

He leaned down, maybe a bit too fast, just as Sarah, who must have been thinking along the same lines, launched up on her toes. The top of her head crashed into his chin, sending a jolt of pain along his jaw.

They pulled back, then kissed awkwardly on the cheeks and backed away from each other, him rubbing his chin, she rubbing her head as the audience erupted in laughter.

"It looks like maybe you need to practice that approach a bit more," Landon joked.

The audience filtered out while the contestants cleaned their stations. Brenda and Dick were stone faced as they gave their area a perfunctory cleaning. Brenda slowed as she passed Raffe and Sarah, her eyes shooting daggers at them both.

"Sorry about your loss," Sarah said. Brenda just glared.

After Brenda was out of sight, Raffe exchanged looks with Sarah, and they both broke into a smile. She held up her fist for a bump. "Hopefully we won't have to field anymore accusations now that Brenda is gone."

"One can only hope." Raffe slid his chef's knives into their sleeves and threw the rag on the counter. Their area was spotless except for the pots and pans in the sink, which the staff would remove and scour in the back kitchen.

They headed to the bungalow, Raffe's heart a little lighter. Another challenge under their belt and a nasty competitor gone. As they walked past Brenda and Dick's bungalow, Brenda came charging out at them with Dick right behind her.

"I know you two are cheating! And I don't care that we just lost, I will make sure you two cheaters don't win! And I'm petitioning for a redo!" Brenda screeched, her arms flailing.

"We aren't cheaters!" Sarah yelled back. Raffe was surprised at how loud her voice could be. She didn't usually yell, but apparently Brenda had gotten on her last nerve.

"Brenda, let's go! Get inside!" Dick pulled on one of Brenda's arms to get her back inside the bungalow, all the time Brenda still yelling, even as the door closed on her shrieks.

"What was that all about?"

Raffe turned to see Dave and Kim.

"Oh, just Brenda going off the deep end, I guess," he replied, shaking his head.

"They accused us of cheating!" Sarah blurted to Kim as the two women started to walk ahead of Raffe and Dave along the path.

"That's ridiculous. You two won fair and square. Great idea on how to cook that octopus, by the way, Raffe."

"Thanks. The searing was Sarah's idea. We make a good team." Raffe had been pretty pleased with the dish.

"Raffe, care to grab a drink?" Dave asked him, nodding toward the beach bar.

Raffe accepted his invitation, and they left the two women sitting on the beach.

The beach bar served the whole resort, but it was fairly empty for late afternoon. They ordered beers in frosty mugs and sat at a bamboo table under a palm tree. The breeze rustled the large palm fronds lazily, and Raffe relaxed into his seat, running his finger down the condensation on his mug.

"So, things are moving fast, huh?" Dave took a sip of his beer.

"Very. It's good, though, I guess. Though the constant anxiety is starting to kill me." Raffe said it jokingly, but it was partly true. He was usually cool under pressure, but the constant daily stress of the challenges plus the sabotage and Brenda's accusations was starting to pile up. Not to mention the kissing.

"Ha! Anxiety! Tell me about it. Try having your entire future riding on this contest!"

Raffe's heart twisted. He didn't know what to say. Dave and Kim had nothing. For them, everything was riding on winning the contest. He had never really thought about the fact that after the show ended they had no home to which they could return.

"What are your plans? For after the show, I mean," he asked, hoping that he wasn't offending Dave.

Dave sighed. "Well, if we don't win, then I guess we just go back to the real world, you know. No more beachfront bungalow. We have a tent on the beach and can stay there. The weather here is amenable to that, well, except during the rainy season. I've been thinking about applying at the resort for a job because they've seen my work now, or at least heard about it. Maybe the fact that I don't have an actual home won't prevent them from hiring me this time."

"This time?" Raffe sipped his beer, the liquid cooling his throat and the tang of hops lingering on his tongue.

"Yeah. I applied for a job here after I was fired from the restaurant. I would have had the job if it wasn't for the fact I didn't have a permanent address here on the island. It's a catch twenty-two. I can't afford an apartment without a job, and I can't get a job without an apartment."

Raffe couldn't begin to pretend that he knew how Dave felt. The fact that Dave and Kim had so much riding on winning the contest made him feel like a jerk.

Whether he won or lost, he'd return to his fancy apartment in New York.

"Now, if we win, that's a life changer right there." Dave took another sip. "Kim and I want to open our own restaurant here on the island. Just a small one, nothing big or fancy. We don't need it to make a ton of money. Just enough for us to pay the bills and get by is fine. We love cooking so much, and love this island so much. It would be a dream come true for the both of us. But enough about me, what about you?"

Raffe told him about his restaurants and his love of the food business. But his usual enthusiasm was dampened by Dave's circumstances. He wanted to offer him a job on the spot, but he got the impression Dave would see that as charity, and he didn't think a guy like Dave would accept charity. The least he could do was pay the bar tab, which he did after another beer and forty-five minutes of good conversation.

As Raffe and Dave parted ways, Raffe began to wonder if his priorities weren't all screwed up.

Veronica sat in her tiny office at her tiny desk beneath the air conditioning vent. It was freezing, but she wasn't cold. In fact, she was a bit heated because of the phone conversation with Tanner. She swung around in her chair, tapping her foot on the floor as she listened to Tanner drone.

"Yes, Tanner, I know how important this is," Veronica said dryly. Did he think she was stupid? I mean, after all, this whole plan had been half her idea. She didn't like being treated like a child, and she didn't need Tanner calling and texting her nonstop, asking what was going on.

"Maybe this just isn't going to happen; the timing is wrong." Veronica made a face as soon as the words came out of her mouth. Had she said that? What was wrong with her? It was that old bag, Gertie. All her talk about karma and her words about being nice were starting to turn Veronica soft!

The thing was, Veronica didn't have the same gusto for ruining lives she'd had a few weeks ago. Maybe that was because her efforts kept being thwarted. But something about Gertie's words rang true, and she really *did* like the old lady.

She respected Gertie, and Gertie understood where Veronica was coming from. She'd been where Veronica was but had persevered and ended up with a great career. Veronica, on the other hand, didn't have any idea what she would do after this show. She wasn't going to be a CEO's assistant anymore, that was for sure, but what else was she qualified to do?

Maybe she *should* stop trying to ruin people's lives and hers would get better. Maybe Gertie had a point about karma.

She rubbed the bandage-covered scratch on her arm absently. It was hot and itchy. She hoped she wasn't getting an infection, as the dishwasher had said. Maybe the scratch was some sort of bad karma for the things she'd been doing to Sarah and Raffe.

But it wasn't fair! She *had* done something good the other day, so why was karma kicking her ass now?

"Nonsense!" Tanner bellowed. "The timing couldn't be better! We've got them right where we want them, in a place to be humiliated. In public! Are you forgetting that thanks to Sarah and her sidekick Marly we both were screwed over? And don't even think of backing out on me. I have proof it was you who switched the dessert, and you won't get a referral if you are fired! And I think we both know Jasper Kenney won't be giving you a good referral from your last job, will he? Do you want to sit in your apartment with no job, gorging on M&Ms again?"

Tanner's smarmy voice made Veronica cringe, but he did have a point. Marly and Sarah *had* gotten her fired, and she had loved that job. Word had traveled fast within the fashion industry about the fact she had been fired, and finding a new job had been nearly impossible.

But she didn't want a job in that industry anymore. Even though she'd only taken the job here so that she could mess up the contest for Sarah, she found herself actually beginning to like it. She enjoyed organizing and keeping things running on time. And she was good at it. The producer had already complimented her several times.

When the contest was done, she hoped to get a

similar job. But that wouldn't happen if Tanner ratted her out.

His remark about her weight stung, but she *had* gained a ton of weight in between jobs. In fact, she was almost as heavy as she had been growing up. But now that she was busy all day running around, the weight was starting to drop off. Another benefit of an active job like this.

"Fine. I'll see what I can do," Veronica said to placate him.

"I *know* what you can do. Use that secret weapon and be done with it." Tanner hung up before she could say another word.

Veronica unlocked the top right drawer of her desk. That was where she locked her purse. Not because she had anything of value but because the "secret weapon" was in there.

She reached in and pulled out a small glass vial. Holding it up to the light, she peered through the clear liquid. Who knew such a strange concoction could exist in a tiny vial like that? It looked as harmless as water.

But it wasn't harmless. It was some kind of mixture that when poured over any type of food would make it taste absolutely rancid.

The problem was getting the chance to pour it over the food without being seen. She should have done it during the favorite meal challenge, but she'd switched the dessert instead, hoping that would be enough to send

Raffe and Sarah home and she wouldn't have to resort to such drastic measures.

Too bad the rest of the challenges didn't really allow for the food to be placed anywhere that she could access without being seen.

The meals cooked went directly from the teams' kitchens to the judges table, and all under the eye of multiple cameras. She'd have to use some major sleight of hand to drop the liquid onto the food *after* Raffe and Sarah had tasted and plated their dishes and before it got to the judges.

If she were caught, she'd be fired and lose any hope of a good reference. She placed the vial back into her purse. That would have to be used as a last resort. There was still another contest to go. She'd just have to figure out a way to ensure they lost without having to resort to the secret weapon.

14

Raffe was still thinking about Dave and Kim when he got back to the bungalow. The excitement he'd felt about the contest up until now had been tarnished by his talk with Dave. Sure, it was exciting to win, but was this really the right way?

Sarah was at the kitchen sink, her golden hair flowing over her shoulders as she sliced limes on a cutting board. Beside her, two ice-filled glasses of soda water fizzed, their bubbles clinging to the sides of the glasses. The air was spiced with the pungent citrus smell. She appeared to be immersed in her task.

Raffe paused to watch her for a second. There was another reason for him to win the contest now—Sarah. Winning would go a long way toward securing her future as a chef. Unlike Raffe, the money mattered to her. And somehow what mattered to Sarah had started to matter to Raffe.

Sarah turned to look at him, her smile lighting her face. "Thank you for sticking up for me earlier, I really appreciate it."

"You don't have to thank me. That's what being a team is all about," Raffe said.

Sarah turned back to the limes, avoiding his gaze. "I'm making lime soda. You want one?"

She tossed several of the limes into one of the glasses, squeezing the juice of a few of the wedges, and held the glass out to him.

Raffe stepped over to take the glass. His hand brushed hers, sending a jolt through him. He looked from the glass to Sarah. She looked up at him, a half smile on her lips. The sun shining through the window highlighted the gold flecks in her amber eyes.

"I've never had anyone watch my back before," she said.

And then, before Raffe even knew what was happening, she stood up on the tips of her toes and pressed her lips against his. It was a whisper of a kiss, so quick he didn't have time to react. Didn't have time to pull her close and make it last longer. By the time he realized it had happened, she'd already bounced back down on her heels and turned back to the limes.

What was that? Probably just a friendly peck, a gesture of her appreciation. Friends did that, right? Sarah had returned to cutting the limes as if it hadn't been important. So clearly she thought the kiss meant nothing.

Raffe was still clutching the drink. He shoved his other hand in his pocket to keep from reaching for her and giving her a proper kiss.

"Well, um, was that practice so we don't knock heads the next time on the show?" Raffe joked.

Sarah laughed and looked up at him, her cheeks flushed. "Just a little thank-you kiss. I feel like we're becoming partners here. Friends."

Right. Friends. The kiss had been simply a *friendly* kiss. Which made sense, because she was probably still with this Tommy guy. She'd go back to him after this was all over and their fake engagement was dissolved.

His throat suddenly dry, Raffe chugged the drink, the prickly fizz of the soda water tickling his tongue.

"I was thinking you might like to grill some food tonight for supper." Raffe put his glass in the sink, careful not to step too close to Sarah.

"That sounds great." She didn't look up from the limes.

"Great. I'll grab something from the community kitchen and meet you down at the grills."

"Okay."

Raffe turned and made a beeline for the door.

SARAH WATCHED from her spot at the kitchen window as Raffe's broad shoulders disappeared down the path. She sliced into the last lime, the knife slipping and cutting her finger.

Damn! That stings!

She sucked on her finger as she walked to the bathroom in search of a bandage, her mind still on the fact that she'd kissed Raffe.

Why had she done that? It had been totally spur of the moment. But in that moment she'd felt so close to him. Maybe it was all his talk about being a team. She'd never been a team with anyone. Certainly not Harley. Maybe Tommy. He'd been the only one to stick up for her until now. Until Raffe.

But it had been a dumb thing to do, and when he didn't respond, she'd had to make light of it. Pretend it was a friendly peck. She'd turned away to chop the lime so he wouldn't see her disappointment. And he'd graciously made that comment about "practicing" to help ease her embarrassment.

Just as well. Things might have gotten out of hand. Once the contest was over, their fake engagement would be over, and the next time she saw Raffe Washburn he'd probably have a gorgeous model on his arm.

Her heart weighed heavy with thoughts of Tommy as she rinsed the small nick in her finger then wrapped it in the bandage. Was Tommy on the island? If so, why couldn't she find him? And then there was her mother's hopeful texts. She hadn't the heart to tell her mother that she'd not heard from Tommy in almost a year. Her mother still thought she could pass messages along.

Maybe the new leads she'd gotten from Kim would pan out. In fact, now was a good time to try them.

Her finger properly wrapped and the sting abating, she headed toward the living room, where her phone sat on the side table. It rang just as she reached for it. Marly.

"I just wanted to check in. I know you had another contest today. Did you guys make it?" Marly asked.

"We did. Actually, we won." She probably shouldn't have been telling Marly this information. They weren't supposed to tell anyone the results of the challenges because the show wouldn't air until a few months after the contest ended. The studio didn't want any of it leaking out. But Marly was her best friend, and she knew she wouldn't blab.

"That's great. But why do you sound so preoccupied? Wait a minute, did you and Raffe kiss again?" Marly's voice rose in excitement at the word "kiss."

Sarah's heart jerked. How did Marly know? Then she realized Marly was referring to the kiss Landon had forced on them after they won the bacon contest, not the one she'd just given him in the kitchen. Marly probably assumed that would happen every time they won.

"No. I mean the audience was calling for us to kiss, but it wasn't really a kiss. We kind of just clonked our faces into each other," Sarah explained.

No way was she going to tell Marly about the other kiss in the kitchen. That would only encourage her to keep trying to fix them up.

"Oh, well, that's a start anyway," Marly said. "So are things going good otherwise?"

"Sure. That crab that kept accusing us of cheating went home today, so things should be smooth sailing from here on out," Sarah said.

"What about Veronica?"

Sarah's gut clenched. Yeah, can't forget about Veronica. Brenda had been a pain in the butt, but Veronica was dangerous. "There hasn't been any funny business in the last two contests. Maybe she's turned over a new leaf."

Marly snorted. "Yeah, right and I'm Coco Chanel. You better watch out for her. The fact that she hasn't pulled something in a while probably just means that she's gearing up for something really big."

"Yeah I guess. We'll keep our eyes peeled."

"Great. I'll check back later."

Sarah disconnected and walked to the front door and peeked out, making sure that Raffe was nowhere in sight. She pulled out the wrinkled piece of paper that she had gotten from Kim when Raffe had been drinking with Dave.

She'd shown Kim the photo of Tommy, but Kim didn't recognize him. She explained that not all the homeless people knew each other. They formed cliques and kind of stuck together. But she'd given her contacts and the local soup kitchens and day labor programs. She knew it was a long shot, but she wanted to call to see if Tommy had frequented any of these places.

The first number on the list went to voicemail. She

left a message saying who she was and that she was looking for her brother. Not a great start.

The next number a real person answered after several rings. She described Tommy. No luck.

She continued to dial the numbers, getting more and more discouraged with each call.

After the last number, Sarah threw the phone on the sofa beside her. No one had seen Tommy. He probably wasn't even on the island. He might never have come here. Probably spent the money she gave him on drugs. She was going to have to resign herself to the fact that she might never find him.

Time to start thinking about her own future. She rummaged in her tote bag and brought out a small notebook. Slumping down, she started to jot some ideas. What would she do once the contest was over? She could always go back to work for Jasper. He had promised her that, but she wanted more. Working all day cooking in the contest and seeing what she could accomplish had shown her that she wanted to work as a chef.

Would Raffe hire her on in one of his restaurants? Would that be awkward? They'd see each other all the time. Did she want that? Did he?

He was opening that new restaurant in New York. Maybe she should ask? She doodled the name Eighty-Eight in the notepad as she tried to visualize what it would be like to be head chef in a new trendy restaurant. Running her own kitchen. Calling the shots. Definitely something to think more about.

She wasn't yet ready to ask Raffe anything, though. She wanted to prove herself first, and she definitely didn't want him giving her a job because he felt obligated. Speaking of which, she didn't want Raffe to come back and ask what she was doing. Not to mention, she still had to clean the limes. She slapped the notebook closed. Better bury it in her bag so Raffe didn't see it.

As she leaned over and shoved the notebook deep into her bag, her phone slipped under the couch cushion so quickly that she didn't even notice.

15

Raffe carried the heavy bag stuffed with food from the community kitchen in his left hand, his right hand holding the phone pressed to his hear. On the other end was the general manager of his new restaurant, and he did not sound happy.

"Darren, I know Edward can be a pain in the ass, but he's like family to me," Raffe said. Apparently Edward had taken his task of overseeing the restaurant construction very seriously.

"Well, if you don't rein him in, you'll end up with things like tofu and bean sprouts on the menu instead of steak and swordfish. And don't even get me started on the new kitchen design he insists on."

Tofu? Since when did Edward like tofu? "What new kitchen design?"

"The old man wants us to move the prep stations over by the walk-in." Darren sounded exasperated.

Raffe tried to picture how that would work. He'd designed the kitchen so the prep stations were at the furthest end of the kitchen, but it made sense to have them near the walk-in. If he'd learned one thing in the contest, it was that you wasted a lot of time running to the cooler when prepping food. Maybe Edward was on to something. "That's not such a bad idea. Go with it."

"Okay, you're the boss, but that guy is driving me nuts."

"I know. Don't worry. I'll be back next week, and you won't have to deal with him anymore."

"Not a moment too soon." Darren disconnected.

Next week. The contest would be done, and Raffe would be back in New York overseeing the final outfitting of the restaurant. Where would Sarah be?

A gecko scurried over the hot stones in front of him as he shifted the bag to his other hand. The bungalow came into view, and a wave of anxiety washed over him. He hoped he'd chosen foods that Sarah liked.

Inside, Sarah was just finishing up at the sink. Two fresh glasses of lime and soda water sat on the counter.

"I hope this is what you wanted." He opened the bag to show her what he'd chosen. Two plump free-range chicken breasts and an assortment of vegetables. "I'll grill, you make the salad and sauce if that's okay?"

"Sounds great." Sarah handed him one of the drinks then grabbed a bag from the counter. "I put some paper plates, utensils, and condiments together."

They headed out of the bungalow toward one of the

charcoal grills at the edge of the beach in the shade of the palms.

It was just before sunset, the sky awash with pinks and purples that highlighted the aqua ocean. Humidity hung heavy in the air, disturbed only by a slight salty breeze that carried the soft sounds of live music from somewhere off in the distance. The tiki torches had been lit, casting a flicker of ambiance over the teak picnic table and benches near the grill.

Raffe fired up the grill while Sarah unpacked the bag.

"I made a lemon-pepper glaze that would be perfect on the chicken." She took out a glass container filled with a yellow sauce dotted with sprinkles of black pepper, and a brush that she used to baste the chicken on the grill. The flames sizzled and jumped as glaze dripped into the fire.

Raffe put mushrooms, onions and zucchini, which he dotted with butter, in a foil pack, sealed it, and placed it on the grill.

The air soon filled with a tangy lemon barbecue scent, and Raffe stood back to sip his drink while Sarah finished the last of the basting.

"Hey, what happened to your finger?" He pointed at the bandage wrapped around the tip of her index finger.

"Oh, I cut it while slicing limes," Sarah shrugged. "It's just a little cut, probably be gone by morning."

"I was surprised at how much food there was in the community kitchen that hadn't been touched. I guess maybe after cooking under pressure every day no one else wants to cook for themselves except for us." Raffe flipped the chicken and flames jumped. He grabbed one of the lemons Sarah had just cut up and squeezed it over the pieces.

Raffe knew Sarah hated to waste food based on the conversations she'd had with Kim and Dave about the homeless people. Sure, wasting the food was stupid, but he wondered why she was so into it. The show had a heavily stocked common kitchen for all the contestants to use for their personal meals. Sarah had asked a few crew members what they did with the extra food every day, but they all just shrugged.

"It's a shame that all that food in the kitchen will go to waste," Sarah said, pulling a red-and-white checkered tablecloth out of the bag she'd packed and grabbing two small rocks to place on either end of the picnic table so the breeze wouldn't keep flapping the ends of the cover up.

"I'm glad we get to just chill and grill a casual meal. All that fancy cooking for the contests is grueling." Raffe removed the chicken from the grill and placed it on plates, handing one to Sarah.

"Yeah, me too. I can't believe how fast everything has moved so far." Sarah pulled another container from the bag and pointed at the foil packs. "I made a balsamic glaze for the vegetables.

Raffe took the foil packs off, juggling them around as he tried to open the hot tinfoil with his fingers. Sarah laughed as he quickly tugged and then pulled his fingers back, dancing around and whistling, "Ouch! Oh! That's hot!"

They dug in to the meal. Even though it wasn't gourmet, it tasted pretty good to Raffe. His thoughts turned to the contest.

"A few more days and we will know if we walk away winners," Raffe said. "Thanks again for doing this. I never really asked you why you agreed to do it. I know you didn't like lying about the engagement."

Sarah didn't look up from cutting into her chicken. "I actually didn't know about that part. Marly only said it was a cooking contest and you needed a partner."

"What? She never told you?"

"Nope. But by the time I found that part out, I was already committed. Plus, Marly and Jasper begged me to do it, and I figured the experience would help me take the next step in my career."

So Sarah *did* want to move into a chef position. Thoughts of the kitchen at EightyEight flashed into Raffe's mind. He needed several chefs. "I thought you liked working for Jasper."

"Oh, I do. Jasper's been great to me. But I don't want to be an administrative assistant forever. I've been in culinary arts school for a few years now. So ultimately that's what I would like to do."

Raffe nodded. Jasper had told him that Sarah had been putting herself through school while she worked for him. It made sense that she wanted to win the contest just as much, if not more, than he did.

"Well, you definitely have impressed me with your skills. And I'm pretty sure everyone else has taken note of them too. I'm sure that when we get back you'll have a ton of job offers. I just hope you remember us little people when you make it big."

Sarah swatted Raffe's arm, laughing. "Yeah, I'll try to fit you into my schedule."

Raffe laughed and felt awkward at the same time, wondering for the first time what it would be like between the two of them when they finished the show and went back to "real" life.

He knew they'd cross paths. Their best friends were getting married, but would they see each other more than they usually did? He hoped so. Should he tell her that? Thoughts of the friendly peck surfaced. No, he might seem too needy or something.

Sarah speared a piece of chicken and looked at him thoughtfully. "Your turn. Tell me why you did this. I mean, you own a bunch of successful restaurants, and I don't think you want to be a chef. So what's the reason?"

Raffe hesitated a moment, unsure if he wanted to open up to her. She cocked her head and widened her eyes. She'd told him her reasons, so it only seemed right for him to do the same.

"Well, I guess I just wanted to accomplish something on my own for once. I actually *am* interested in being a chef—well, having the same knowledge, anyway. In my restaurants I know the business side and am respected for that, but when it comes to the kitchen, the chef usually has the final say. I'd like to be able to manage the kitchen and have the background to back me up, you know? I would love to be able to teach them some things instead of the other way around. At times I feel they think I'm only there because of the family money. And I'm sick of carrying that around. I've been doing it my whole life." Raffe looked down at his plate, unable to meet her eyes. "For once I want to achieve something that can't be bought with my father's money. Something all mine."

"I think that's great. I mean, if we win the Chef Masters competition then obviously your chefs will know that you know what you're talking about. Just don't consider putting any Peeps and M&Ms-themed desserts on your menus and you should be okay."

They both laughed at that. Raffe shook his head.

"I'm still not sure who is trying to sabotage us. It's pretty crazy if you think about it. But no one has tried anything the past two challenges, so maybe those really were accidents," Raffe said.

"Maybe, but I still say we need to be on guard. I do not trust Veronica."

"Yeah, good point. We'll watch each other's backs."

Sarah smiled and nodded, holding Raffe's gaze. His heart warmed at the special friendship forming between them.

They finished dinner and cleaned the area before heading back to the bungalow. Raffe wondered if he should suggest they go to the bar for a drink. Just as he was about to ask, Sarah made a suggestion.

"Should we watch a movie?" she asked, scrolling through the options.

"Sounds good." Raffe rummaged in the refrigerator, coming up with a bottle of wine. He held it up to her. "Pinot Grigio?"

Sarah nodded. "Sounds good."

Raffe grabbed two wine glasses and sat on the sofa. He opened the wine and poured both glasses.

"How about this?" Sarah paused at a horror movie.

"Don't tell me you like horror movies?" Raffe wouldn't have pegged her for the type, but then there were a lot of things about Sarah that surprised him.

"Like? No. Love? Yes! Especially the older ones. You know, *Friday the Thirteenth, Halloween.* Those types."

"*Texas Chainsaw Massacre.* That's the best. Because it's based on a true story. And I mean the original movie, none of that remake bull," Raffe said.

"You mean this *Texas Chainsaw Massacre?*" Sarah teased, pointing to the movie that was an option for the online movie selection.

"Yes! Let's rent it." Raffe settled back with his wine glass. There was something about sitting here with Sarah that felt comfortable. Homey. Maybe it came from cooking together, from the compatibility they'd achieved in the kitchen, but hanging out with her was effortless. Like hanging out with his best friend.

They watched the movie, laughing and screaming

together throughout it, with Sarah at one point almost crying she laughed so hard. When the credits finally started rolling, Raffe was sad it was done.

"That was the most I've laughed in a long time," Sarah said, wiping a tear from her eye.

"Me too." Raffe turned to Sarah, happy. During the movie they'd moved closer to each other. Raffe's arm was extended along the top of the sofa. Sarah right next to him. Close enough to kiss. Raffe inched even closer then dipped his head, capturing Sarah's lips with his.

Her lips were soft and warm, and she kissed him back. He sensed a hesitation, though, and broke the kiss. "This was one of the most fun nights I've had in a while."

"Umm, yeah, it was great."

Raffe couldn't read the tone in her voice. Had she liked the kiss or not? She didn't slap him across the face, but she didn't jump his bones either.

That was probably for the best. Because they both had to stay in the bungalow together and keep their act together for the rest of the contest, he decided to play it safe.

He touched the tip of her nose with his index finger then moved away. "Well, it's late, so I guess I'll use the bathroom first. We should turn in so we can be fresh for whatever they throw at us tomorrow," he said, stretching and then standing.

"Yeah, good idea." Sarah cleaned up the kitchen while Raffe used the bathroom. Then she took her turn while Raffe pulled out the sleeper sofa. He got between the sheets and lay there, waiting for her to come out of the bathroom.

Would she say anything? Come to him? Did he want her to? Things could get complicated, and he really didn't need that. Plus, he sensed Sarah was the real deal. The kind of woman you took things slow with.

The bathroom door clicked open, and his heart skipped. He heard her footsteps shuffle into the hall then hesitate. Then she whispered, "Good night."

"Night," Raffe replied. And then Sarah closed the bedroom door, leaving Raffe and his thoughts alone.

16

TJ paced in front of his boss's old metal desk, the floor squeaking under his sneakers. He'd been called in, but he had no idea why. He kept to himself for the most part, which wasn't hard to do considering he typically worked the night shift. It was beyond busy all of the time, and there wasn't much time for conversation.

So what could he possibly have done wrong? The only people he ever talked to were Gertie and that angry blonde. Maybe she had reported him for something.

"This is highly unusual, and there's no protocol for it."

"For what?" TJ asked, having no clue what his boss meant. Had someone seen him stealing that food a few days ago?

"Well, you received a tip today. Someone left some cash in an envelope for you."

"Huh? For me? Are you sure?" TJ asked, perplexed as to who would do such a thing. He was a dishwasher. No one really even knew him aside from the others who worked in the kitchen. Besides, this wasn't exactly the type of gig where one received tips.

"Yes, I'm quite sure. It doesn't have your name on it, but it does say, 'For the skinny tall dishwasher.' You're the tallest dishwasher and definitely the skinniest. Here."

TJ took the envelope and opened it. Inside were five crisp one hundred dollar bills. He looked up at his boss.

"I don't get it. Why? I mean, I just wash the dishes around here."

"Well, I don't know either. Maybe you have a secret admirer or something. Put it in your pocket and don't tell the others. I was torn between giving it all to you and splitting it between the kitchen staff. I opted to give it to you because it was meant for you. Now go along back to work."

TJ walked out of the office, scratching his head. Who would give him five hundred dollars? That money was equal to almost three weeks of scrubbing pots and pans. The island paid extremely low wages. He put the money in his wallet and decided to just call it good luck.

17

Sarah stretched her arms above her head and grabbed her blue-and-white striped light cotton hoodie from the back of the chair as she tiptoed out of the bungalow. It was early, and Raffe was still asleep on the couch.

She'd had a great time watching the movie with Raffe. They'd laughed together, and she'd felt some sort of connection forming. And he'd kissed her! And not a friendly peck or a head-clonking kiss... a *real* kiss. But what did it mean? She'd been so stunned she hadn't known what to do.

And then it was so awkward because they were living together. She wasn't the kind of girl who jumped into bed after the first kiss. Was that what Raffe had expected? It had been hard to tell, but she'd thought she sensed a change in him after she'd come out of the bathroom and not hopped under the sheets with him.

She hadn't slept well. Conflicting feelings about Raffe had caused her to toss and turn. But now it was morning, and Sarah loved mornings. A walk would help clear her head, and there was a long path that meandered around the resort she'd been meaning to check out.

She also had wanted to call Upper State Rehab without Raffe overhearing, just to get the prices for treatment. She knew they would be astronomical. Tommy had no insurance, but if she and Raffe won the contest, she'd have $250,000, and that had to be enough. She'd spend it all on Tommy if she had to. *If* she could even find him.

The morning air was balmy. The surf pounded a steady beat for her to keep pace with. The path was surrounded by lush vegetation, dew glistening on the leaves and flowers. Colorful birds flew from flower to flower, some serenading her with their raucous calls and lilting chirps.

As she followed the trail, her mind wandered again to the conversation she had had with Raffe the night before. He'd opened up to her about his reason for wanting to win the contest. She knew it had more to do with proving himself to his father than to do with gaining more expertise for his restaurants.

A twinge of guilt pinched her gut. *She* hadn't been completely honest with *him*. She hadn't told him about Tommy and the fact that she hoped to use the contest winnings to send him to rehab.

Raffe hadn't turned out to be anything like she'd

expected. He wasn't the rich playboy jerk that he appeared to be on the surface. He was just a regular guy who wanted to be accepted for who he was. A normal guy. A guy Sarah wouldn't mind getting to know better. Had she blown that chance by not telling the truth?

Thoughts of the truth reminded her that she wanted to call the rehab facility. She reached into the pocket of her hoodie for her phone.

Her heart skipped. It wasn't there. She could have sworn she put it there last night.

Maybe her back pocket.

Nope.

Shit! Where was it? Slowing her pace, she turned the pockets of her hoodie inside out, where was that damn—

Ooof!

"Watch where you're going, you moron!" Veronica shrieked, throwing her arms in the air, her phone clutched in one hand, blood oozing from beneath a bandage on her arm.

"It was an accident, Veronica. Sorry if I crushed any of your M&Ms." Sarah was usually much more diplomatic, but she was in no mood for Veronica's shit this morning.

Veronica was the last person she wanted to see right now, or any time really. And they weren't supposed to even be talking to each other. Sarah quickly looked around to make sure no one saw them. All she needed was someone to happen along the path and see them. Thank God Brenda had already been sent home. Still, she couldn't help but let Veronica know that she suspected what she was up to.

"By the way, you can stop trying to get me and Raffe disqualified from the show. It won't work. We're smarter than you."

"I've done no such thing! I wouldn't waste my time trying to do that. Although, I *was* a bit surprised that someone as hot as Raffe Washburn would choose you, the invisible mousy girl, as a fiancé. But it looks like maybe he's found someone else?" Veronica smirked as she shoved her phone in front of Sarah's face, showing her the photo of Raffe and Gina hugging.

Sarah stood in silence as Veronica walked away, her hideous cackle drowning out the birdsong.

She walked a few feet and sat down on one of the carved granite benches placed along the path, trying to make sense of the photo Veronica had just shown her.

There was no denying it, photos don't lie. Raffe and Gina had something going on. Of course, she'd seen Gina flirting with Raffe the entire time, but he had acted as though he wasn't interested.

Had he been lying about that? Was he the type to go after a married woman? Maybe he was the type who went after *any* woman. Maybe last night had simply been another attempt at a conquest for him.

But something about that didn't ring true. The Raffe she'd come to know wasn't like that. Then again, she wasn't the best judge when it came to men. Take Harley, for example. Look at what a jerk he'd turned out to be.

And she never wanted to feel the pain she'd felt over him again. Yep, best to stick to her plan to never get involved. That was the smart thing to do. Good thing she hadn't given in to her impulses and let things get out of hand with Raffe last night.

She grabbed for her missing phone again, wanting to call Marly. Wait! Had she left it on the couch last night? She walked back to the bungalow, the image of Raffe hugging Gina flashing across her mind.

———

RAFFE SAT up on the sleeper sofa, rubbing the stubble on his chin and squinting at the sunlight beaming in from the sliding glass door. He saw more sunlight peeping out from Sarah's bedroom door and guessed the curtains must be open.

Standing up, he grabbed his shirt, threw it on, shuffled to Sarah's bedroom door, and poked his head inside.

"Sarah?" he asked, looking around. No response. She must have left already.

He padded to the coffee maker and brewed a cup then sank down on the sofa, thinking about the night before.

Had he been wrong to kiss her? He didn't think so. He had a pretty good radar when it came to women. Then again, the women he usually dated were nothing like Sarah. Maybe his radar didn't work on her. Maybe the connection he thought he'd felt was just a happy vibe because they were doing well in the contest.

Maybe he was letting their living arrangements go to his head.

Sarah probably just got caught up in the moment. Better to play it safe around her. The last thing he wanted to do was make a fool of himself.

Bzzz.

Something vibrated under his butt.

What the heck? He moved over and picked up the cushion. A cell phone was under it. The display was unlocked, showing the last few text messages.

...Of course I love Tommy anyway.

And then her mother's texted reply: *"Honey, you have to tell Raffe about Tommy, it's not fair."*

Raffe's heart sank. He hadn't meant to eavesdrop, but now that he'd seen the messages, he couldn't unsee them.

Sarah really did have another boyfriend. Yet she'd kissed *him*. Twice! So much for her sweet and innocent act. Raffe should have known it was too good to be true, someone who was smart, a great cook, down to earth, and appeared to like him for himself and not his money. Ha! Sarah was a cheater just like Lauren.

He sighed. What right did he have to be judging her? It wasn't as if they were really engaged. And it was just a few kisses. So what?

He couldn't very well expect her to break it off with her boyfriend over a fake engagement. And it made sense her mother would think it wasn't fair that Sarah was engaged to Raffe and still stringing Tommy along.

The thought of spending the morning alone in the

bungalow with her lost its appeal. He needed some space to clear his head.

Grabbing a piece of paper, he wrote Sarah a note and then changed and headed to the conference center to get ready for the next contest. Only two more to go, and this farce would finally be over.

"HELLO?" Sarah yelled as she stepped inside the bungalow. Raffe was nowhere to be found.

Her eye caught the shiny surface of her cell phone on the coffee table.

Did I leave it there?

Beside it lay a piece of paper. A note from Raffe.

Sarah—found this under the cushions. Headed over to the conference center.

Sarah turned the note over in her hand. That's it? Why would he leave without her? They weren't supposed to be there for another twenty minutes.

Maybe this was his way of telling her that the kiss meant nothing, that their *friendship* was only temporary.

Well, if that was what he wanted, then so be it. She didn't have much respect for a guy who fooled around with married women anyway.

But she still had a contest to win, and she was going to do her damnedest to make sure she got that money for her brother. She grabbed her phone off the table and headed toward the conference center.

18

Raffe's knives were all sharpened to perfection, the countertops gleamed, and all the cooking utensils were in place. The only thing missing was Sarah. Where was she?

"Hi." Sarah hurried in and grabbed her apron, turning her back to him as she put it on.

Was it his imagination, or was she acting a bit stand-offish? She probably regretted kissing him. Whatever. He wasn't here for kissing, he was here to win a contest.

Glancing over at the other contestants, he caught Gina's eye. She and Tony huddled together, his arm slung around her shoulders. They were probably discussing strategy. They appeared to be doing much better since Raffe and Gina had spoken a few nights ago. He winked at her and smiled, happy that his advice had seemingly helped.

A hush fell over the audience as Landon grabbed the

microphone and signaled for the cameras to start rolling. Raffe set his knives aside and stood still, his nerves on high alert as he waited for the announcement.

"Teams, the next challenge will test the one skill every chef should possess, the delicate art of baking pastries. You will create your own pastry dish. It can be a meal or a dessert. Time starts *now!*"

Raffe followed Sarah as she raced to the walk-in. He hoped the mild panic he felt didn't show on his face.

"It might be better if you took the lead on this. I'm a bit rusty on pastries," he said as she shoved butter, sugar, flour, and baking powder at him.

"Okay," Sarah replied, sounding preoccupied as she reached up on the shelf for some pears.

"So, are you thinking about doing a tart maybe? A pear tart?" Raffe asked as he watched Sarah lay the pears on the cutting board. It would be nice if she were a bit more communicative. He hoped he wasn't going to have to be a mind reader for the entire challenge.

"Yes. Slice those up."

Raffe took a pear and starting dicing it.

"What are you doing? No! Not like that. In long slices. This is a pastry we are making, right? Cut it the long way, like in layers."

Sarah's voice was tight with frustration, and Raffe tried not to let his own exasperation show. The producers lived for drama, but he couldn't let them see him getting upset, or worse, unsure of what the hell he was doing.

He reached for another pear and sliced it correctly, watching Sarah as she began filling a mixing bowl with flour.

"Is that too much flour? We don't want the dough too thick."

"No, it's fine," Sarah replied, adding even more flour to the bowl, making Raffe wonder if she had done it just to spite him.

"More butter," Sarah demanded, nodding her head toward another bowl.

"Are you sure? I just put some in, and I'm pretty sure it was enough." Raffe wasn't an expert on pastry crust, but he had made enough to know the correct amount of butter. Sarah was using so much butter and flour that she could bake enough pastries for Napoleon's army.

"I don't know. I thought I didn't see enough go in," Sarah replied curtly, taking the bowl and adding more butter. She slowly added the flour to the butter and turned on the mixer. After a few minutes she dumped a clump of dough out of the bowl and started to roll it. "Well, great. This is too thick."

Raffe held his tongue and instead looked around at the other teams. They all seemed to be working in unison, and the room was filling with that sugary sweet bakery smell, signaling that they were way ahead of him and Sarah.

They continued on, arguing over whether or not to add water or milk to thin the dough (they did not, which Raffe knew was a mistake). After arguing and bumping into each other more than once by the end of the contest, both of their faces were bright red, a result of frustration rather than the heat of the oven and the overhead studio lights.

"*Time!*" Landon yelled just as Sarah pulled the clumsy-looking pear tart from the oven.

Raffe looked at the tart, it's lightly browned crust the only positive factor about its appearance. There had been far too much dough, and the pear filling barely peeked over the top of the fluted crust. Memories of failed projects in his eighth-grade home economics class came to mind. This was not the work of a top chef.

Crew members whisked the dishes to the judges, who sampled them, picking at the crusts with their forks to test the flakiness.

Raffe and Sarah exchanged worried looks when it came time for the judges to test their tart. The crust was anything but flaky. It was a thick dough, like a pretzel. Durkin's pursed mouth told Raffe he was unimpressed with their creation. He barely took a bite before moving on to taste the next contestants'.

"We have the final decision." Landon announced holding his hands up dramatically to hush the audience. "This was a close call. You should all brush up on your pastry-making skills! Raffe and Sarah, your tart was tasty, but the dough was much too thick. Rob and Brian, your tart was overcooked. The inside fruit was hard and the bottom crust was burnt. Everyone else's was adequate. The rest of you will continue on."

Raffe's stomach swooped as the other chefs sighed in relief. Either he and Sarah or Rob and Brian would be going home.

Landon turned to Raffe and Sarah. "Team One, your crust left a lot to be desired, but your filling was superb." He swiveled to Rob and Brian. "Team Six, no aspect of your dish was palatable. Therefore, Rob and Brian, you are eliminated." Landon dropped his hands down, and the audience went wild.

A wave of relief washed over Raffe. They'd barely squeaked by. As the other teams celebrated, he turned to Sarah, but she had turned away from him to fiddle with her knives, ignoring him completely. What was up with her?

Was she angry with him? If she was, she should have set it aside and not let it affect the contest, which it clearly did. They'd almost lost!

But why did the fact that she was ignoring him sting so much? That had nothing to do with the contest. Feeling foolish for allowing his feelings for her to get out of control, he angrily gathered the trash to bring to the compacting room.

19

V eronica was giddy with excitement over Raffe and Sarah's loss. And judging by what she'd seen, they were seriously off their game.

Something was wrong in paradise! Maybe it had been the photo of Raffe hugging Gina that she had shown Sarah. She hoped so. Whatever it was, now was the time to twist the knife in deeper and hope they'd screw up on their own.

If not, then she would have to take drastic action and use the liquid. But there were only two challenges left, and the producers were planning to throw a monkey wrench in the works to keep the chefs off balance. She'd have to plan carefully, because if it looked like they were going to win, she might have to deploy some fancy foot-work to sabotage the dishes before tasting. If she was fired for using the secret weapon, so be it.

She scratched at the cut on her arm. Stupid thing, was it getting worse?

Raffe suddenly appeared in the hallway outside of her office, lugging a trash bag toward the compactor room. She scurried out from behind her desk and nonchalantly stepped in his way.

"Oh, hi, Raffe. Sorry about that last loss. It's too bad, really. I mean, I think you're the best chef, even if Sarah…" She let her voice trail off dramatically.

Raffe's eyes narrowed in suspicion. "Even if Sarah what?"

"Oh, nothing. I mean, face it, she's right anyway. You're only here because your daddy has so much money and your name is well known… You don't really have any cooking capabilities. She's not even trying anymore because she figures you already paid to have your team win."

"What!" Raffe exclaimed. "Is that what Sarah said?"

Veronica smirked, knowing that she'd landed on a sore spot. She didn't even have to answer Raffe's question, because he'd already turned away. Hurling the trash bag into the compactor, he stormed down the hallway, leaving her standing there smirking and scratching her arm.

Yes! She'd ruined his day! She should feel overjoyed, but for some reason it didn't feel as satisfying as she'd thought it would.

She turned to see Sarah coming down the hall. Maybe

winding Sarah up would give her that euphoric feeling she usually got when she ruined a person's day.

"Oh, hi, Sarah!" she smiled coyly despite Sarah's look of suspicion.

"What do you want, Veronica? We aren't supposed to be talking. You know that. Or do you have more photos to show me?"

"Don't take your loss out on me. You and Raffe screwed that up yourselves. The two of you bumping into each other out there like idiots. Anyway, I don't know why you'd bother doing a good job given the circumstances."

"What do you mean, 'given the circumstances'?" Sarah asked in an irritated tone, brushing aside a strand of hair that had fallen down from her bun.

"Well, what's in it for you if you win? A job at one of Raffe's restaurants if you're lucky?"

Sarah tried to push past her, but Veronica inched closer, like a predator closing in on prey.

"There's the grand prize money, that's what there is," Sarah said, shoving her way past.

"Not for you," Veronica replied, laughing.

Sarah turned around sharply. "What? What do you mean by that?"

"In the entry form that you signed, it shows that, if you win any money, it all goes into Raffe's bank account. I mean, maybe it's a joint checking account you two love-birds share. I'm sure you saw that when you read the rules? Couples only, and the prize goes to one bank account. It *is* strange, though. All the other couples had *both* names on their bank accounts. I heard Raffe talking to one of the crew members about how his daddy wouldn't give him any more money to open more restaurants, so he needed this money bad. I'm sure you know all this, though. After all, you're engaged to the man."

Sarah's face turned bright red, and she stormed away, leaving Veronica alone to bask in her triumph. But Veronica didn't feel very triumphant. She heard a tsk-ing sound behind her and whirled to find Gertie shaking her head, disappointment plastered on her face. She must have heard everything. Gertie wheeled off to her office.

The urge to explain why she'd done what she'd just done overwhelmed her, and she started toward Gertie's office. Gertie shook her head then grabbed a long stick and used it to slam the door closed.

Veronica stood in the hall staring at the closed door, a lead balloon settling in her stomach and her arm itching and burning as if infested with fire ants.

She turned and slowly walked to her own office. She should have been bubbling with victory but instead felt as though she'd just let down her only friend.

20

Raffe stormed into one of the bars inside the conference center, sat down, and ordered a shot of Jameson.

"Rough day?" the man nursing a beer next to him asked. His white brows shot up over clear blue eyes. His face was tanned, and muscular white hairy arms stuck out from his faded red T-shirt.

"Yeah, you could say that," Raffe replied, grabbing the shot glass from the bartender and shooting it back as he used to in college.

"Let me guess, it's about a woman, right?" The old man laughed and ordered another shot for Raffe as well as himself.

"Yup. A woman who I didn't want to like in the first place. Someone I started to trust and then *boom*, she turned out to be a liar, just like the last one!" Raffe tossed back the second shot as quickly as the first.

"Well, what do ya need her for? Nothing! Better to just walk away from her." The old man held his shot glass up and then drank it back, a bit slower than Raffe did but still impressive for his age.

"You're right. I don't need her, or any woman for that matter. Much better off without them! Things always end up messy when a woman is involved."

"I'll drink to that!" the old man exclaimed, downing his beer and ordering another round.

Raffe grabbed a beer too and took a long swig. He didn't need anyone, and certainly not Sarah. She had led him on the whole time. She didn't even think he could cook! Screw her.

SARAH PACED BACK and forth inside the bungalow, furious at herself for even agreeing to enter the stupid contest in the first place.

What had she been thinking? Opportunities like this don't ever come for people like her. She should have known it was too good to be true and that Raffe was a jerk who would just screw her over.

He had needed her to enter the contest because it required a couple. He never intended to split the money with her. He probably had already rigged it so they, or *he*, would win, so he could take the money! So much for doing things the right and honest way and *earning* respect as a chef. That had all been a lie too.

The bungalow door whooshed open, and Raffe walked in, smelling of whiskey and bad decisions and reminding her of so many times with Harley. Sarah had been down this road before and had no desire to retrace her steps.

"You! You're a liar and a cheater!" he yelled at her, waving his arms around like a madman and slurring his words.

"Me? *Ha!* You're the liar and cheater! You are not who I thought you were at all!"

"Who did you think I was? Someone only made of money who needed his daddy to get onto the show? Someone who can't even cook, so now you're not even going to try to win this contest with me because I've already rigged it to win?"

Sarah rolled her eyes at him, her face bright red. His drunken babbling made no sense.

"That's all that's important to you! *Money*! You can just never have enough of it, right? You're no different than Harley. It's all about money and screw anyone or anything that gets in your way. Who cares if people get hurt, right? You planned to take all the money if we won anyway! Don't try to deny it! You know what you can do? Take this ring and shove it!"

With that Sarah jerked the fake ring off her finger and hurled it at his head. Raffe ducked, and it pinged loudly off the sliding door behind him.

Sarah stormed out of the bungalow. Raffe Washburn and this stupid contest could go screw!

21

Raffe's eyes jerked from the ring on the floor in front of the door to the slamming front door. What had just happened?

The argument had gotten out of control fast, and he just now realized some of what Sarah had said made no sense.

What did Sarah mean that he planned to take all the money if they won? Where did she get that stupid idea? Didn't she know he already had money, his *own* money? And who was Harley, and why did she think Raffe was like this lying Harley dude when *she* was the liar? She was probably going off to meet Tommy or Harley right now!

He paced inside the bungalow for more than an hour, the whiskey slowly wearing off as he pumped himself full of black coffee.

The ring winked at him from the floor. He picked it up, noticing its weight. Wide and gaudy. No wonder

Sarah kept fiddling with it. He stuffed it in his pocket. Not that he'd have another use for it, but he couldn't see throwing it out.

Now that the booze had worn off, he wondered if he'd been a bit harsh with Sarah. She wasn't even his girlfriend. She could do whatever she wanted to with whomever she wanted. She'd been off base to insinuate he was money hungry, but that was no excuse for calling her a liar and a cheater. He'd acted like a jerk.

Raffe collapsed onto the sofa, the ugly truth sinking in. He *had* pulled strings to get on the show. He had used his connections and lied about being engaged. He hadn't paid anyone off or rigged the show, as Sarah thought, but he still wasn't completely innocent. Maybe he *was* the cheater Sarah had said he was. The thought stung like a slap in the face.

He owed her an apology at the very least.

His head spinning, he headed outside for some fresh air. He walked slowly, following the path to the small row of resort shops. In the window of one, something caught his eye.

He stood mesmerized on the sidewalk, tourists in splashy outfits carrying colorful shopping bags zigzagged around him. Making up his mind, he stepped inside.

Raffe returned to the bungalow an hour later, disappointed that Sarah was not there.

Walking out of the sliding glass doors, he looked around the beach and saw a cluster of red-striped beach chairs in a circle by the water. Hands shot up from two of them, waving him over. It was Dave and Kim.

"Is everything okay? We saw Sarah earlier, and she seemed out of sorts," Dave asked, motioning for Raffe to sit.

"Yes. No. I mean, we had an argument. You know how it is. I don't know. Maybe we just aren't meant for this whole marriage thing. She's probably better off with Tommy." As he spoke, Raffe realized he spoke as if they really were engaged. He'd love to be able to tell Kim and Dave the truth, but he still held out hope that Sarah would join him and they'd win the contest. He couldn't spill the beans after making it this far.

Dave and Kim looked at each other.

"Tommy? What do you mean Sarah's better off with him?" Kim asked, confused.

"Well, he's her ex. I guess. I don't honestly know. She never really mentioned him, but she's been preoccupied the last few days, and I saw some texts with his name on them. It's either him or someone named Harley."

Kim laughed.

"Raffe, Tommy is Sarah's brother. He's been in trouble for years. On drugs. Sarah's last boyfriend, Harley, was a drug dealer and got Tommy hooked. The whole family thought he was an investment banker, but it turned out he was one of the largest heroin dealers on the East Coast. Tommy has been homeless the past few years. Drifts in and out of Sarah's life. She hasn't heard from him in months. She had a feeling he was here on the island and even looked for him one night. How is it you two are engaged but you don't know all of this?"

Suddenly everything clicked into place. Was that why Sarah had snuck out of the resort? To find her brother? And that's why she needed the money from the contest. To help her brother. And the text messages about Tommy weren't about some ex-boyfriend she still loved. They were about her brother!

He'd made a huge mistake. He needed to find Sarah now and apologize. To put things right. To make her see that he wasn't a shallow cheater and that she'd come to mean more to him than just a way to win a cooking contest.

"Thanks, guys, I gotta run!" He turned to go and almost ran into Jim, the show's crew member. Crap! What did he want? Was he being summoned to Scott's office again? Judging by the look of panic on Jim's face, something was definitely going on.

"Hi, guys. Everyone needs to be on set in five minutes! The final contest is happening. Chop, chop! Move along!"

Raffe, Kim, and Dave looked at each other. "What? Now?" all three asked in unison.

"It's not scheduled until tomorrow," Kim pointed out.

"Yes, *now*. You know how the producers like to throw

you off balance with surprises. This is one of them. Adds a level of stress. Head over to the conference center immediately, please. If you aren't there on time, you're out of the contest."

A jolt of panic seized Raffe. "Wait! There's an issue. Sarah isn't here!"

Raffe ran his hands though his hair, looking anxiously down the beach. Where had she gone? But instead of Sarah, he saw Landon Barkley strolling toward them, his hands in the pockets of his tan chinos, a smug look on his face.

"I see you've been informed of the schedule change. I hope this isn't stressful or inconvenient," Landon said, obviously delighted at their stressful inconvenience.

"One of the chefs is missing," Jim said.

Landon frowned. "Missing?"

"Well, not missing," Raffe looked over Landon's shoulder and across the beach, hoping to catch a glimpse of Sarah. "Sarah went out."

"Out?" Landon tilted his head quizzically. "She must be on the premises. No one is allowed to leave."

Raffe sighed. Maybe the guy would take pity on him. "We had an argument, and she ran off, but if you just give me twenty minutes, I know I can find her and—"

"An argument, you say?" Landon looked positively giddy.

Raffe nodded.

"And she stormed off?"

Raffe nodded again, a sinking feeling in his chest.

Landon clapped his hands together. "Marvelous! There's conflict! Drama! And audiences love conflict and drama! The ratings will be sky high! Come with me, Washburn. You'll finish the contest on your own."

SARAH STORMED DOWN THE PATHWAY, the phone pressed to her ear. She wasn't even sure where she was going. She just wanted to get as far from Raffe as she could. "I just want to come home. I'm done. This whole thing is a joke, Marly."

"Calm down. I don't know why he'd call you a liar and a cheater, so I don't blame you for wanting to come home. But what about the contest? The money?"

Sarah had told Marly that she needed the money, but not the whole story. All Marly knew was that Sarah's brother had some issues and that the money would be a huge help.

"I don't know. I'll figure something out. I just can't stay here and pretend anymore. I've had enough." She stopped short. "Great! I just realized I don't even have any of my stupid stuff with me. Now I need to go back to the stupid bungalow."

"Maybe you should wait until you calm down a bit," Marly suggested.

But Sarah was beyond calming down. She said goodbye to Marly and stomped back toward the bunga-low, cursing under her breath. She'd left in a huff, not thinking about packing. She wanted to get away from the island right now. Maybe she should just leave everything, because going back meant she'd have to face Raffe. Too bad her purse, credit cards, and identification were still in the bungalow.

At least she'd made a dramatic exit. It was too bad her aim with the ring had been off and she'd missed Raffe's head.

As she turned the corner to the bungalows, Gina almost bowled her over. The woman seemed to be in a hurry, maybe on her way to some sort of clandestine meeting with a lover. Probably with Raffe. But why was she carrying her knives?

"Where are you going?" Gina asked, a panic-stricken look on her face.

"Why do you care where I'm going? Don't worry, it's not anywhere with Raffe. You can have him all to yourself now." Sarah felt childish as soon as the words came out of her mouth. That was so not like her. This thing with Raffe really had her frazzled.

"What are you talking about?" Gina's eyes were round with innocence.

"Oh, cut the crap, Gina. I saw the photo of you and Raffe. Does your husband approve of that?"

The confused look on Gina's face morphed to laughter.

"Oh, Sarah, really? You think I put the moves on Raffe? He was giving me advice on my marriage. He saw me crying. I've had nothing but problems with Tony for months leading up to this contest. In fact, it's a huge reason I entered us in the contest," Gina said. "I don't care about winning. I wanted to be alone with Tony. I thought it would be a good bonding opportunity for us. Instead, Tony ignored me almost the whole time! I spilled my guts to Raffe. I was at my wit's end, and he really helped me out."

"He did? But you were embracing. I saw a photo."

Gina made a face. "I don't know anything about a photo. I mean, I think I hugged him after he helped me out, but the whole time he was giving me advice he gushed on and on about you. He's obviously crazy about you." Gina stepped past her. "But why are you wasting time about that now? We need to get to the conference center for the last challenge."

"Last challenge? That's not until tomorrow."

"Not anymore." Gina hurried off, her gold bracelets clanking as she called over her shoulder, "They made a last-minute change. It's happening *now!*"

Sarah stood in the path, her brain trying to catch up with the conversation. Was it true that Raffe had only been helping Gina? The hug had been an innocent gesture? Gina had seemed sincere. She wasn't angry or stuttering over lies like someone trying to cover up.

And then Sarah thought about who had shown her that photo—Veronica. She should have known better than to give the photo any credibility. And who had told her that Raffe was keeping the money all for himself? Veronica! She'd been so befuddled about Raffe's supposed affair with Gina that she'd lost all common sense and believed Veronica's lies.

She ran toward the bungalow. She'd been a complete and utter idiot! She had to catch Raffe and apologize before the challenge, before the relationship they'd started to build was ruined.

The bungalow was empty. Crap! Had Raffe gone on to the contest? She rushed back out and broke into a sprint for the conference center.

The doors at the chef's entrance were locked. She pounded on them with her fist, yelling for someone to let her in.

"Ma'am, this is a live show. You can't come in," a security guard advised as he approached from behind.

"I'm on the show! *See?*" she fired back, showing him her badge. "You have to let me in!"

The guard eyed her skeptically, his eyes flicking from the badge to her face. Then, after what seemed an eternity, he got on his radio as she tried to decipher the static gibberish squawking out of the device.

"Sorry, but you won't be allowed into the chef's area," the guard said. "The producer says it's off limits now. The challenge is almost ready to start. You can sit with the audience if you want."

Sarah stared at him, her eyes stinging with tears. She was too late? What now? Would they automatically lose?

She slowly nodded... She would sit in the audience. He pointed her toward the audience entrance, and she made her way inside, praying that Raffe could forgive her and that they hadn't already been disqualified because of her foolish actions.

***

STUPID PRODUCERS! Veronica popped four M&Ms into her mouth, barely chewing them before swallowing.

After all the work she'd put into trying to pull Sarah and Raffe apart so they forfeited the contest, that damn Landon Barkley let Raffe into the final challenge on his own!

He still had a chance to win, even if his cooking skills sucked in comparison to that mealymouthed Sarah. But she'd been counting on getting them into such a snit about each other that one of them took off and they'd be disqualified. At least she'd been successful with half her plan.

Veronica reached into her purse and pulled out the vial of clear liquid and slid it into her pants pocket while heading toward the cooking area.

Passing Gertie's office, she poked her head inside. She hadn't seen Gertie all day. She missed her snarky comments. The old bat was kind of growing on her. In fact, she might even be the closest thing Veronica had to a friend. It was comforting to know someone who had grown up with a similar struggle, even if she was one hundred years older.

Something was wrong. Veronica's heart skipped as she noticed the photos were gone from the walls. None of Gertie's awards were on the bookshelf. There was nothing but bare, crappy rental furniture in the room now.

But today was the final challenge. Surely Gertie wouldn't have gone anywhere before the conclusion. Maybe she'd changed offices? If the air conditioning vent was anything like the one in Veronica's office, this one might have been too cold for the old woman.

Veronica grabbed the arm of a crew member who was walking down the hall and pointed to Gertie's empty office. "Where's Gertie?"

"Oh, I'm sorry. You didn't hear? Gertie's gone."

"What the hell do you mean gone? Where? To another office? Which one?" Veronica snapped at him, scratching the cut on her arm, which now itched furiously.

"Umm, sorry. I mean she's no longer with us." The crew member gave her a knowing look before pulling away and scurrying down the hall, leaving Veronica staring into Gertie's empty office with a hollow in her heart.

22

R affe stood alone in the kitchen, the hair stuffed under his chef's hat damp with sweat. The bright studio lights blinded him but not enough that he couldn't see the audience gawking at the one chef who had to complete the challenge alone.

Landon had made a big deal of Raffe going it on his own. He'd cited a lovers' quarrel, which had been a big hit with the audience. Some women had even volunteered to stand in. Apparently Landon had been right about drama being good for ratings.

As if it wasn't bad enough to summon the teams to the kitchens before they were mentally prepared, the judges threw another curveball at them. There was to be a quick elimination round, and then after that, only two teams would remain. Those two teams would battle it out for the ultimate victory immediately after.

Could he pull this off by himself? He was hyperaware

of the empty space beside him. The space where Sarah should be. Sarah was the one who acted quickly on her feet. Sarah had a good sense of food combinations. He needed her.

Raffe's eyes darted from the knives to the utensils to the counter. He took a deep breath, getting into the zone.

You can do this.

He had to do it. For Sarah. He owed it to her. And now that he knew why she needed the money—for her brother—he was determined to get it for her.

He glanced at the other contestants. Gina and Tony looked happy, their arms around each other. A feeling of satisfaction swelled in his chest. He'd helped them reconnect.

The hopeful looks on Kim and Dave's faces made his heart clinch. They had the most to lose. Of all the teams, they'd probably worked the hardest to earn the title.

Raffe looked back at his own station. If he won, it wouldn't mean nearly as much to him. He hadn't paid anyone off to rig the contest, so he'd finally have the satisfaction of earning something on his own, but somehow, looking at Kim and Dave, the thought of winning now felt hollow.

Maybe there was a way everyone could win?

"And now, the dish for the elimination round." Landon had grabbed the microphone and beamed at the camera. "Each team will have thirty minutes to create the best dish they can with five ingredients." Landon looked pointedly at Raffe. "It's going to be a tough one for one of our teams. Let's see if he can do it alone."

The audience tittered, obviously excited about the added challenge of a one-chef kitchen.

"And it starts now!"

Raffe froze with indecision then suddenly knew what he was going to cook. One of his favorite dishes. He loved it because it was so simple, with only five ingredients, yet the taste was worthy of a five-star restaurant.

He grabbed a pot from under the sink and filled it half full then rushed it onto the burner, the water sloshing dangerously close to the brim. The burner lighted with a familiar click, click, click, and he turned to rush to the walk-in refrigerator before his hand was even off the knob.

He grabbed Gruyère, cheddar, fresh truffles, cream, and handmade bow tie pasta. Using the bow tie pasta over elbow macaroni for the fancy macaroni and cheese recipe would dress up the dish.

He raced back to his station, throwing the pasta in the water before mixing the cream and cheese. He seasoned everything perfectly with salt and pepper and a dash of paprika—seasonings didn't count toward the five ingredients. It was a simple dish, but when combined with the truffle, the taste was absolutely decadent.

Raffe was in the zone, not paying attention to the audience or Landon or the other chefs as he moved quickly about the kitchen. Gone were the nerves he'd felt in the previous contests. He was finally in his element.

"Time's up!" Landon yelled just as Raffe placed a sprig of parsley on top of the macaroni and cheese.

A staff member took his plated dishes and brought them to the judges' table. Raffe stood still, pulse thudding, as each judge raised a brow at the dish then took a tentative spoonful. Durkin leaned back and closed his eyes then dug in for another bite, and the tension in Raffe's shoulders eased. The critic liked it. That was a good sign.

The judges went through their tasting routine, taking bites from all the dishes, bending their heads together in whispered consultation. Then finally they gestured for Landon. He approached the table. There was more whispering before the host wheeled around and nodded at the camera.

Raffe's heart thudded as Landon strolled closer to the stations. "We had some very unusual dishes in this very unusual competition. And one team was down to just one chef. Can one chef in the midst of a lover's quarrel out-cook his happy couple counterparts?"

The room was silent.

"Raffe, I admire your persistence. You've done an admirable job on your own, but..."

Raffe's heart swooped. He was being cut out of the competition. He'd lost.

Landon continued, "...someone has to go home." His head swiveled to Gina and Tony. "Gina and Tony, I'm sorry. Your dish, though delectable, fell short in the seasoning. Too salty. You're out of the competition.

Raffe, Kim and Dave, you will compete for the title of Chef Master!" Landon screamed the last words out.

The crowd cheered.

Raffe did a double take. He was in? Kim and Dave bounced over to his station and hugged him. He was in. He'd done it!

Gina and Tony came over to congratulate the two remaining teams.

"Sorry you guys didn't make it." Raffe shook Tony's hand.

"Winning would have been great, but we got something even better than that from this contest." Tony slipped his arm around Gina's shoulder and gave her a squeeze. "Didn't we, honey?"

"We did." Gina mouthed a silent "thank-you" to Raffe, and his heart swelled.

"We'd better clean up before the next round." Dave wiped his hands on his stained apron, the stress evident on his face. "Good luck."

"You too." Raffe turned to his sink, putting the dirty pots on the cart that would haul them to the back kitchen where they did most of the dishwashing. He made his way to the storage area to grab more pots, anxiety building with the knowledge that the final contest was only a few minutes away.

On his way back, he caught a glimpse of bleach-blond hair skulking around the walk-in cooler. Veronica? Was she sabotaging something back there? He was about to investigate when Landon's voice jerked his attention back to the performance area.

"We have a special guest in the audience, everyone. It's Sarah! I guess these two love birds might make up after all!" Landon's words elicited laughter and hoots from the audience.

Sarah was here?

Raffe's heart thudded as one of the cameras zoomed in on his face. His eyes scanned the audience, locking on Sarah's. She was seated in the front row, behind the judges. She smiled tentatively and gave a little finger wave.

She wasn't angry! Raffe broke into a huge grin, and Sarah's smile widened in response.

He could tell by the look in her eyes that she wanted to be on stage with him, that she knew he wasn't the jerk that she had said he was earlier. He had no idea what had changed her mind. Maybe something had happened after she had stormed out of the bungalow. Maybe she had talked to someone. Raffe didn't care. All he cared about was that she'd come back for him. And now he knew that was what mattered to him more than anything.

Something clicked deep inside him, and Raffe felt a renewed determination to prove himself to Sarah. He wanted more than anything for Sarah to have the money she needed for her brother.

Something inside him had changed. Now it wasn't only about proving himself to his father and others. He wanted to be a better man for Sarah. And a better man doesn't cheat and lie his way into contests. Raffe couldn't change what he'd already done, but…

Landon appeared in front of him, his arms raised, pointing at the camera to start rolling. "And now, the moment you've all been waiting for."

The room grew quiet, and the audience shifted in their seats.

"It's down to two teams… well one and a half."

The audience chuckled.

"But Raffe is cheered on by his lady love!"

A camera swung in on Sarah.

"Will that be enough to help him win?"

The camera swung back to Raffe.

"And now, the final challenge. The challenge that will determine who becomes the next Chef Master and who goes home with egg on their face…" Landon gave one of his by-now-familiar dramatic pauses. "And I do mean egg, because this challenge is to cook your best quiche!"

Quiche! Yes! Raffe was a veritable quiche master. What a lucky break.

"But there's a catch," Landon said. "You must use all the eggs in your carton, no more and no less. *And* you must use all of the milk in one of these containers."

Landon waved his arm dramatically at a table behind Raffe that held three tall test-tube-like containers filled with milk. Each container was filled to a different level.

Raffe squinted at the containers. They were so tall and thin it was impossible to tell how much milk was in each. His gaze swiveled to the container of eggs on his counter. Five eggs. The ratio of eggs to milk was critical for quiche.

He glanced over at Dave and Kim's eggs. They had seven eggs.

Shit! Which tube held enough milk for five eggs?

"That's right, folks, this will test your culinary judgment. There is a container there perfect for each team, so you each have a chance to acquire the exact amount of milk you need. *If* you choose the right one. Now, the question is, who gets which container?" Landon gave his Cheshire cat smile to the camera. "I think we'll have a race to determine that."

Landon stepped to an area ten feet from the table with the milk vessels and indicated a yellow line on the floor. "Raffe, Dave, Kim, please join me behind this line."

Raffe exchanged uneasy glances with Dave and Kim as they took their places behind the line.

"When the challenge starts, you'll run to the table and grab the vial of milk that you want to use for your eggs," Landon explained. "Dave and Kim, you pick one vial. Raffe, you pick one. You'll be racing against each other, obviously, but remember, you must use the entire vial and all your eggs!"

Raffe eyed the vials. This could make or break the contest.

"Ready. Get set. Go!"

Raffe took off toward the table.

"You have ninety minutes to prepare a fully baked quiche!"

The three of them arrived at the table at the same time. Raffe reached for a vial. No wait, he didn't want to take the one that held the correct amount for Dave and Kim's eggs! Dave and Kim whispered to each other, grabbed the middle vial, and ran back to their station.

Raffe took the container on the left and ran back to his station, turning the oven to four hundred degrees and then rushing to the pantry for the ingredients for crust.

Crust wasn't really his thing. He usually made crustless quiche, but he knew the crust would add a savory element the judges would enjoy. If only Sarah were in the kitchen. She'd bang out the crust in no time. But it was all up to him now. He closed his eyes and tried to remember what she'd done to make the pear tart crust. That one hadn't come out right, but he knew why. He could use the right mixture of ingredients to make the perfect crust.

He glanced up at the audience, searching for Sarah. She perched on the edge of her seat, watching him. As their gaze met she nodded and gave him a thumbs-up. He smiled and did the same, his confidence blossoming as he returned to the crust.

Once his crust was assembled, he shoved it in the oven to bake before running to the refrigerator for the quiche ingredients. Broccoli, ham, cheese, nutmeg. He remembered seeing Veronica back here. Had she sabotaged something? It didn't matter. He had a plan, and whatever Veronica did couldn't hurt him. It might even help.

He raced back to his station, glancing at Kim and Dave. They looked frazzled. Kim pointed at the mixing bowl and Dave shook his head.

The worried looks on their faces halted Raffe. Such stress. And fear. The contest—the money—meant everything to them. It would give them the break they needed. The only thing he wanted or needed was Sarah, and winning the contest wouldn't guarantee that, but he had an idea what might.

He went back to work on his dish. He poured the milk from the tube into a bowl, eyeing it. He'd need two and a half cups of milk for the five eggs. It looked about perfect.

At Dave and Kim's station, the couple were eyeballing their egg-to-milk ratio, and they did not look happy.

Raffe looked at the bowl of milk in front of him and then at the eggs in the container. He started cracking eggs into the milk, making sure to return the shells to the container as instructed. He spread them out so they were clearly visible. Wiping his hands on his apron, he glanced up to see if the judges were watching. He had a plan.

Raffe mixed the quiche and then set it in the oven. It would bake for an hour and would come out just in time. He noticed Kim and Dave hadn't gotten theirs in the oven yet. They were cutting it close.

He wasn't allowed to leave the area or the scrutiny of the judges while the timer was ticking, so Raffe used the time to put together an arugula salad with strawberries, and a hollandaise sauce to complement the quiche.

Getting lost in the work, he was comforted the few times he glanced up to find Sarah watching, silently cheering him on from the audience.

He had just enough time to get the quiche out of the oven and plate individual slices with the sauce and salad when Landon yelled, "*Time!*"

Raffe stepped back and looked at the plates just as the kitchen staff whisked them away to the judges' table, but not before he saw the pie-shaped pieces of quiche starting to ooze over on the plate.

Raffe smiled. He was happy with the final results.

The judges didn't seem happy with either dish. Raffe could feel the panic radiating off Dave and Kim. Their quiche had looked a bit rubbery. They must have chosen the wrong milk.

Durkin summoned Landon to the judges and whispered something. Landon then strode to Raffe's station and looked in the egg carton. "Team One, you used all your eggs?"

"Of course. The shells are there." Raffe pointed.

Satisfied, Landon proceeded to Kim and Dave. "Team Eight, your shells are all present?"

Dave lifted the egg carton, and Landon peeked in then turned to the judges and nodded. "Judges, do we have the final results?"

The judges frowned down at their dishes and then huddled with Landon.

After a long pause, which contained much gesturing to the dishes on the part of the judges, a grim-looking

Landon stepped forward to make the final announcement.

"This was a difficult decision." He scowled at Raffe and then at Kim and Dave. "The judges were not wowed by either dish as the consistency of the quiche was not perfect from either team."

Raffe glanced at Sarah. Her eyes darted from Kim and Dave to Raffe. He almost felt what she was thinking, and he felt the same way. She wanted them both to win.

"Raffe, the flavoring in your dish was excellent. The spices added just enough zing to your dish to make it interesting," Raffe's heart twisted as Landon turned to Kim and Dave. It sounded almost as if the judges favored Raffe's dish best.

"Kim and Dave, your ingredients were unique and refreshing." Landon frowned. "But your quiche was a tad rubbery."

Raffe heard a disappointed sigh from Kim, and his heart twisted even more. Kim and Dave were about to lose everything.

Landon turned back to Raffe. "On the other hand, Raffe, your quiche was runny. Neither dish was perfect, but given the overall scoring of flavor, presentation, and consistency..." Raffe held his breath through the usual dramatic pause. "The winner of the Chef Masters title and the five-hundred-thousand-dollar grand prize is..." Landon paused as the camera swiveled to Raffe then to Kim and Dave then back to Landon. "Team Eight, Kim and Dave!"

The audience and staff erupted in applause. A blizzard of confetti rained down from the ceiling. The audience, except for Sarah, rushed to Kim and Dave's station. While Raffe watched the melee breaking out around Kim and Dave with a big smile on his face, he saw Sarah break from the crowd and run toward him.

"I'm sorry you… we… didn't win. You must be—" Raffe turned toward her, and her face turned quizzical. "Happy?"

Raffe's smile widened. He *was* happy. The win meant so much more to Kim and Dave than it would to Raffe, and everything he needed was right beside him.

"Yes, I am happy." He opened his arms, and Sarah stepped into them.

"You were wonderful! The crust looked amazing and the ingredients delicious." She hugged him tighter. "I don't understand why—"

Crack.

Sarah stiffened and pulled back a few inches before noticing the gooey stain spreading from Raffe's apron pocket.

"You lost on purpose?"

He smiled sheepishly. "I figured they had a lot more riding on it. See, I'm not the money-grubbing asshole you heard I was. And besides, some things are much more important than money."

Raffe barely got the words out before Sarah threw her arms around him and planted a kiss on his lips.

SARAH'S HEART swelled as she hugged Kim and Dave, congratulating them on their win with Raffe by her side.

She was overjoyed for them but a little disappointed that she and Raffe hadn't won, mainly because she needed the prize money for Tommy's rehab. She forced herself to push that to the back of her mind.

Raffe had done the right thing. Winning this contest would be life changing for Kim and Dave, and they deserved it. Besides, she didn't even know where Tommy was. She would have to find him first and then find a way to pay for rehab.

She didn't know what was going to happen between her and Raffe, but she felt they had the beginnings of a relationship. Not a fake one, something real. What, exactly, she had no idea, but with both of them returning to New York, maybe she'd get the chance to find out.

She and Raffe had compared notes briefly while she'd tried to clean the broken egg out of his pocket inconspicuously before they pushed their way through the crowd to congratulate Kim and Dave. Raffe had explained in whispers that he'd tried to pick the wrong milk container, but when he'd actually chosen the right one, he'd had no choice but to hide the egg and spread the shells of the other eggs throughout the container so it looked as if he'd used them all. He hadn't wanted to be obvious about throwing the contest, because he wanted

Kim and Dave to have the pride of having won fair and square. He knew Dave wasn't the type to accept charity.

They'd also compared notes on what had caused their big argument: Veronica. Sarah should have known that she'd lied to both of them to cause disharmony in an attempt to make them lose.

But where was Veronica now? As far as they could tell, she hadn't made any attempt to sabotage the final contest. That had Sarah worried. It wasn't like Veronica to leave it up to chance when she clearly wanted them to lose.

23

Passing a dumpster on her way out of the conference center, Veronica tossed the vial of clear liquid away. It wouldn't do any harm in there. She paused for a minute, realizing that she'd done the right thing for the first time in a long time.

A smile started to spread across her lips.

Ding!

She looked at her phone. Tanner. The smile faded as she read his text.

What's going on? Have they lost yet? Don't forget, I can ruin you.

"Screw you, Tanner."

She blocked his number and continued out of the conference center to her room. She needed to pack and get the hell out of there. The show was over, and so was her job.

Good riddance to it. Sort of. She'd enjoyed parts of it.

The organizing. The fast pace. The satisfaction of being the one who made things run smoothly. And even some of the people. Like Gertie. The backs of her eyes pricked as she thought of the old lady. Gertie would have been proud that Veronica had taken the high road and not sabotaged the final challenge.

But Gertie was the only one she'd really miss. Except maybe that annoying floppy-shoed dishwasher. Messing with him had made the day a little more fun. Maybe she should swing by the kitchen and try to be nice to him before she left.

Nah, she didn't want to see him again, and besides, she'd left him that tip. That was enough. That should make for some good karma for her too. He deserved a tip. She knew the show didn't pay much, and even though he was annoying, he had worked his ass off at all hours to make sure the set was stocked every day by five a.m. And that had made *her* look better. That would look good on her letter of recommendation from the show's producers.

She knew he needed the money. His clothes were raggedy, and he looked as if he didn't get enough to eat. Plus, it wasn't her money; she had petty cash left over, and she'd rather see it go to him than back to the show's fat-cat producers.

She glanced at her arm. Funny, it had stopped itching and was no longer red. Karma?

Squeak. Squeak. Squeak.

What the heck? Veronica whipped around, her heart

soaring when she saw Gertie wheeling herself along the path.

"You're alive?"

"What? Of course I'm alive! I'm not that old, for crying out loud," Gertie said.

"Someone said you were no longer with us. I thought they meant you had died!"

"Those idiots. I quit! I'm starting my own gig. Gonna be based in New York City. What about you?"

Veronica's mind raced. New York. Her home.

"I'm headed back home, which is New York. How's that for a coincidence?" She grinned at her new friend. Maybe there really was something to this karma thing.

"TO CHEF MASTERS!" The clicking of glasses echoed in the courtyard, followed by laughter.

Raffe and Sarah had joined Dave, Kim, Gina, and Tony at the outdoor bar near their bungalows for a final celebration. The briny ocean breeze chased away the humidity, the sun warmed Sarah's shoulders, and everyone was happy.

Gina and Tony held hands like teenagers, and Gina again thanked Raffe for his words of advice.

"We may not have won the contest, but we reconnected with each other, and that's more than money can buy," Gina said.

Sarah flushed, embarrassed that she'd thought Gina

and Raffe had something going on. She'd apologized to Gina, who had simply laughed it off.

Kim and Dave were ecstatic, having gone from homeless to five hundred grand richer overnight. The smiles on their faces lifted Sarah's heart, as did the knowledge that Raffe had sacrificed his own goal of winning the contest so they could have the money.

"And we're opening a restaurant right here on the island," Kim said.

"We're going to make sure we have jobs for qualified people even if they don't have a permanent address," Dave added.

"And we're going to make sure we don't waste any food. Unused portions will go to a special food bank for the homeless," Kim said.

"That's great. About time someone did that," Sarah sipped her rum punch and settled back in her seat. Her happy thoughts tinged with sadness. Would Tommy be one of the homeless people they fed? Was he on the island or somewhere else? And if she ever found him, how would she get the money for his rehab?

"We hope you'll all come to the grand opening," Dave said.

"Wouldn't miss it for the world." Raffe pulled out a business card and handed it to Dave. "Let me know if you need any help. I know a thing or two about the business side of running a restaurant."

They finished their drinks and said their goodbyes

after exchanging contact information and slowly made their way toward their bungalows to pack.

A feeling of melancholy mixed with nerves descended on Sarah. She and Raffe wouldn't be living together any longer. Would he ask if he could see her? Would they date? It was all so suddenly awkward.

She hauled her suitcase out to the living room. Raffe stood looking out the sliding glass door. She glanced out, one last look at the gorgeous aqua seas before heading back to the city.

Raffe turned and pulled something out from his pocket—the ostentatious phony engagement ring that Sarah had thrown at him.

"I don't suppose you want to put this back on?" he asked, waving it back and forth.

"Oh God! No!" Sarah replied, laughing. "No offense, but that can be thrown in the trash for all I care. It's not my style."

"Well, how about this one then?" Raffe pulled out another ring, this one a tiny stone flanked by brilliant, sparkling sapphires.

Sarah froze. "Wha… wha… what's that?"

The ring was identical to the one her grandmother had, the one she'd said she would want if she were to pick her own engagement ring. But surely Raffe wasn't asking her to marry him. She liked him, but it was too soon for that kind of commitment.

Raffe laughed as he grabbed her hand and slid the ring

on. "Don't worry, it's not what you think. It's just a promise. A promise of a good friendship and maybe more. I saw it in one of the shops downtown and thought of you. I want you to have it as a memory of this crazy time we spent together." He reached into his other pocket and handed her a piece of paper. "Oh, and this is for you too."

Sarah unfolded the paper and smiled at the yellow smudge of egg yolk on one of the corners. Inside was the contact information for a rehabilitation center in upper New York state, one Sarah knew as one of the best in the country. And very expensive. It was a great gesture, but unfortunately they hadn't won, so there was no way she could help her brother get there now.

She looked up at him with questioning eyes. How had he even known about Tommy?

"Before you say anything, I know about Tommy. I know you agreed to be in the contest to help pay for his rehab. And I ruined that for you by losing on purpose. So I want to give you the money to pay for his rehab. But, there's a hitch, and you sort of have to repay me."

Sarah didn't know what to say. She was suddenly suspicious. She'd never accept that kind of money unless she could repay it, but that would take a lifetime on her salary.

"Hitch?" she croaked out.

"Yes. You can repay me by coming to work at Eighty-Eight, the new restaurant I'm opening in New York. I want you to be my executive chef."

TJ ASKED the cab driver to pull beneath the bridge and keep the meter running. He got out, stretched, and looked out at the ocean for the last time. It had felt weird riding in a cab, even weirder that he was going to the airport, but the five hundred bucks he'd gotten allowed him to buy a plane ticket. He was heading home with some of the meager savings he'd accumulated from the job.

The show had been the only work he'd been able to get in months. He hadn't cared about the show or the work, he only wanted to save enough to make the final payment on the debt he owed and get back to New York.

He didn't even know when the show would air or the chefs who had competed. He'd kept to himself and hadn't made any friends. Well, except Gertie and that feisty blond lady who was always yelling at him. Not that he could call her a friend. Still, there was something about her. What did it matter? He'd never see her again.

He jogged over to a beat-up tent and poked his head inside. Grabbing his worn, dingy duffel bag, he turned around and walked to the small group of people huddled in a circle.

"Hey, guys, it's been real. Someone can have my tent. See you around!" They each shook hands and hugged. No one asked where he was going or what he was doing. That's how the homeless community worked. No questions, just good wishes.

As he returned to the cab, someone came up behind him, clapping a hand on his shoulder. He turned to see one of the homeless people he'd become sort of friendly with. Bob, though TJ didn't think that was his real name.

"Hey, good luck, man," Bob said.

"Thanks." TJ held out his hand and clapped Bob on the shoulder. "You too."

"Keep safe, TJ. Someone came by looking for you, but we didn't let on that you lived here." Bob nodded and then turned with a little wave and headed down the beach.

Good man.

Many in the homeless community had something or someone they were running from, and TJ was no exception. It was agreed upon that, if anyone came looking, they kept their mouths shut.

But TJ wasn't worried about the people looking for him anymore. He'd sent the final payment for the drug debt he'd accumulated before he got clean. That's why he'd been working every job he could and living in a tent instead of an apartment. Every penny went toward paying that debt.

And now, thanks to that five-hundred-dollar tip, he even had enough money to get back home. He knew a halfway house that would put him up until he found a job and was able to save enough for a security deposit. The prospect of getting an apartment and starting over lightened his step.

He could even finally contact his sister, Sarah. He

knew he'd hurt her when he'd dropped out of sight, but he'd been terrified the bad guys would hurt her in order to get the payment from him, so he'd broken all ties, even going so far as to change his last name. He only hoped she could forgive him.

He got back in the cab and asked the driver to take him to the airport, looking out the window at the island he had called home for almost a year.

Maybe he'd look up Gertie when he got to New York, see if she had any work for an ex-druggie accountant.

———

TANNER DURCOTTE HUNG up his phone then wrung his hands. His contact at the show had just informed him that Sarah and Raffe had lost and were heading back to New York.

His joy over their loss was tinged with confusion. His contact said that Sarah and Raffe seemed happier than when they first arrived on the island. How could that be? Had that idiot Veronica somehow made things worse? He couldn't ask her because she hadn't answered his calls or texts in more than a day.

He wouldn't be surprised if Veronica had screwed him over. You couldn't trust anyone these days. And if his contest informant was right, Veronica had totally gone rogue. She hadn't even tried to use the secret weapon!

He glanced at the framed photo of his wife. Emily

would not have approved of what he was doing. Emily would have told him to be nice, to do unto others as he would want done to himself. Emily had believed in all that golden rule jumbo, and look where that had gotten her. Stage four cancer and gone in six months.

That had proved to Tanner that there was no such thing as karma. If there were, Emily would still be alive. She was the sweetest, kindest person he'd ever met. And when she died, part of Tanner died with her. The nice part. Now all he had left was bitterness and anger.

And that bitterness and anger needed to be fed, so Tanner wasn't about to give up on his quest to hurt those who screwed him and caused the failure of his fashion company. He would have his revenge. Now he had a new enemy to add to his list—Veronica—and rumor had it *she* was also coming back to the city.

"That's okay," he said aloud to himself. "Come back to New York. I'm waiting."

****

WILL Veronica really change her ways? Find out in book 3 of the Corporate Chaos series - join my email list to get an email about my latest book releases:

http://www.leighanndobbs.com/leighann-dobbs-romantic-comedy/

If you want to receive a text message on your cell phone for new releases, text ROMANCE to 88202 (sorry, this only works for US cell phones!)

Join my Facebook Readers group and get special content and the inside scoop on my books:
https://www.facebook.com/groups/ldobbsreaders

Other Books in This series:

In Over Her Head (book 1)

ALSO BY LEIGHANN DOBBS

Magical Romance with a Touch of Mystery

***

Something Magical

Curiously Enchanted

Romantic Comedy

***

Corporate Chaos Series

In Over Her Head (book 1)

Contemporary Romance

***

Reluctant Romance

Cozy Mysteries

Lexy Baker Cozy Mystery Series

* * *

Lexy Baker Cozy Mystery Series Boxed Set Vol 1 (Books 1-4)

Or buy the books separately:

Killer Cupcakes

Dying For Danish

Murder, Money and Marzipan

3 Bodies and a Biscotti

Brownies, Bodies & Bad Guys

Bake, Battle & Roll

Wedded Blintz

Scones, Skulls & Scams

Ice Cream Murder

Mummified Meringues

Brutal Brulee (Novella)

No Scone Unturned

Cream Puff Killer

Mooseamuck Island Cozy Mystery Series

* * *

A Zen For Murder

A Crabby Killer

A Treacherous Treasure

Mystic Notch

Cat Cozy Mystery Series

* * *

Ghostly Paws

A Spirited Tail

A Mew To A Kill

Paws and Effect

Probable Paws

Silver Hollow

Paranormal Cozy Mystery Series

***

A Spell of Trouble (Book 1)

Spell Disaster (Book 2)

Nothing to Croak About (Book 3)

Cry Wolf (Book 4)

Blackmoore Sisters

Cozy Mystery Series

* * *

Dead Wrong

Dead & Buried

Dead Tide

Buried Secrets

Deadly Intentions

A Grave Mistake

Spell Found

Fatal Fortune

Sweet Romance (Written As Annie Dobbs)

Hometown Hearts Series

***

No Getting Over You (Book 1)

***

Sweetrock Sweet and Spicy Cowboy Romance

Some Like It Hot

Too Close For Comfort

Regency Romance

* * *

Scandals and Spies Series:

Kissing The Enemy

Deceiving the Duke

Tempting the Rival

Charming the Spy

Pursuing the Traitor

The Unexpected Series:

An Unexpected Proposal

An Unexpected Passion

Dobbs Fancytales:

Dobbs Fancytales Boxed Set Collection

————

Western Historical Romance

***

Goldwater Creek Mail Order Brides:

Faith

American Mail Order Brides Series:

Chevonne: Bride of Oklahoma

————————————

ABOUT THE AUTHOR

USA Today Bestselling author Leighann Dobbs has had a passion for reading since she was old enough to hold a book, but she didn't put pen to paper until much later in life. After a twenty-year career as a software engineer with a few side trips into selling antiques and making jewelry, she realized you can't make a living reading books, so she tried her hand at writing them and discovered she had a passion for that, too! She lives in New Hampshire with her husband, Bruce, their trusty Chihuahua mix, Mojo, and beautiful rescue cat, Kitty.

Her book "Dead Wrong" won the "Best Mystery Romance" award at the 2014 Indie Romance Convention.

Her book "Ghostly Paws" was the 2015 Chanticleer Mystery & Mayhem First Place category winner in the Animal Mystery category.

Don't miss out on the early buyers discount on Leighann's next cozy mystery - signup for email notifications:

http://www.leighanndobbs.com/newsletter

Want text alerts for new releases? TEXT alert straight on your cellphone. Just text COZYMYSTERY to 88202 (sorry, this only works for US cell phones!)

Connect with Leighann on Facebook:
http://facebook.com/leighanndobbsbooks

Join her VIP Readers group on Facebook:
https://www.facebook.com/groups/ldobbsreaders